B

S0-AAA-254

FRONTIER
STEEL

FRONTIER STEEL

Nevada Carter

WALKER AND COMPANY
NEW YORK

First published in Great Britain 1965
Reprinted 1981

First published in the United States of America
in 1982 by the Walker Publishing Company, Inc.

This edition published in 1984.

ISBN: 0-8027-4008-1

Library of Congress Catalog Card Number: 81-71198

Printed in the United States of America

10 9 8 7 6 5 4 3 2

I

He was almost a courtly man the way he tipped his hat and softly spoke, the way he smiled easily and laughed noiselessly with his blue-steel eyes, and this was part of the competence a man acquired on the frontier where other men were sensitive to slight and quick to react to insult.

Below the open throat of his shirt the skin was bronzed from violent suns and the hide was solidly packed with stringy muscle built up over the years by hardship, work, and a life that was seldom mild.

He might have fit into any other society on earth except that he was part of a restless environment which hadn't ceased seeking some vague, far horizon since the first wagoneers had pushed westerly across the muddy Missouri, and if Fate had played a trick and had set him down somewhere else, he probably wouldn't have remained; he'd have been drawn to the West as though by a magnet simply and solely because, like many another, regardless of where he might have originated, he was, and always would remain, a part of the tapestry of new worlds, far places, and raw frontiers.

His name was Wayne, Dallas Wayne. He was two inches over six feet tall and tipped the scales at one hundred and ninety pounds. He had reddish-brown hair and blue eyes, and although with men like Dallas Wayne it was always difficult to guess their age correctly, he was thirtyish. Perhaps thirty-five or thirty-eight. He had met life head-on, had triumphed in nearly all those raw encounters and owned twenty sections of good land. Twenty sections was nearly thirteen thousand acres. A man who came out of a wintry, blood-red sunset with nothing more than his horse, his gun, lariat, courtly manners and his inward ways, had to possess more than the ordinary rider had, or else he'd never have acquired riches in so short a space of time.

Dallas Wayne had been around Virginia City less than four years. Rumour said he'd been lucky at cards, but only the very naïve believed a man could be *that* lucky. A more nearly probable assessment was the one Viriginia City's bankers and successful merchants held to; that Dallas Wayne had come to Nevada with saddlebags full of Confederate gold. This would at least have accounted for his spectacular success in four short years, but actually, no one knew with any degree of certainty just how Dallas Wayne *did* acquire all that land, all those thousands of cattle, except that he'd paid cash for the land over the years, and had imported the herds, presumably also paid for in cash.

Of course he was a Texan. Before he ever opened his mouth people guessed that much about him. Old Texas families had a way of making rock-sure their offspring would never forget the pride of origin that went with being a Texan: they named their children for national heroes like Sam Houston or Davy Crockett or Travis. They also named them for places like San Saba or Chisolm—or Dallas.

But there was another heritage that marked Texans

far from home, their Texas way of speaking; the way they used a soft *r*, the way they occasionally flavoured their speech with Spanish words or Spanish curses, the way they had of rarely raising their voices, and this latter characteristic had filled many an unmarked cow-camp grave, because in a land of violent, vociferous men, that soft-spoken Texas drawl just didn't ever seem to register deadliness.

But it was the manners of Dallas Wayne—along with his frontier competence, his land and cattle, his sprawling ranch-house, his fiercely loyal Texas riders, and of course his bankroll—that made the merchants of Virginia City defer to him, and which also inspired all the matrons with unmarried daughters to scheme for his marital entrapment.

However, without ever really seeming to, courtly, long-legged Dallas Wayne had thus far managed gracefully to sidestep every snare, and do it without giving offence, because it was always hard to be angry with a man who swept off his hat in purest cavalier style and wickedly smiled deeply into the flustered eyes of the mothers of eligible daughters because the mothers were never sure that Dallas hadn't secretly flirted with them. He was a handsome man; every middle-aged woman privately cherished the wickedness of being desirable, but being desirable to such a lordly person as big Dallas Wayne, well, a thing like that could make the most scheming mother forget her own daughter and preen just a little, herself.

But there was another side to Dallas Wayne. He knew people. Knew how they thought and reacted and most of all, he knew how they concealed the issues which in varying degrees motivated them all, the issues of greed, cupidity, selfishness, graspingness, deceitfulness, and while folks speculated upon his phenomenal successes, attributing these things to everything under the sun but the correct reason, Dallas went his way quietly smiling, quietly mannerly, and quietly acquiring the land, the buildings in town, the notes and deeds and mortgages which formed and sustained his compounding wealth, and also, since wealth was power, his growing weighty stature in Nevada Territory.

One fall a cowboy heading down out of the cold country passed through Virginia City, caught sight of handsome, big Dallas Wayne standing in front of the red-brick bank talking to some men, and hadn't moved for a full two minutes after Dallas and his friends moved leisurely on into the bank building. Then that cowboy had strolled over to the Green Door, a saloon that catered to rangemen, sombrely drank until he was fully mellow, and had turned to stand with his back to the bar and expound to all within hearing distance of the great exploits of Hoods Texans during the War of the Rebellion.

Except that Virginia City's population was predominately Yankee, this might have gone down all right. Plus that fact, though, that the war had been over nearly two decades, and like all veterans, time had softened the most bittered memories leaving only the glory to be recalled, and consequently the blue-belly veterans were all for hoorahing this drifter out to the edge of town.

Just one thing kept them from it. The cowboy broke into peals of laughter in the midst of his recitation concerning the way ex-saloonman General Hood and a handful of his Texans had skunked a thousand Yankee soldiers, captured four hundred of them and turned back that spearheading invasion of Texas.

" What in hell," growled a grizzled ex-Yankee soldier, " is so funny about that, Texas?"

The cowboy dashed tears from his eyes, had another drink, held up an imperious hand for silence, then he said, still with a hint of hard amusement in his voice, " Why hell, boys, you got the man right here in your town, all dressed up in a clean white shirt an' doeskin gloves an' shiny black boots who cut the throat of the unarmed secret service agent who was tryin' to get through to Gen'l Lee with Abraham Lincoln's proposal for a truce."

For a long while no one said anything except for a little sigh of soft whispers from the younger men in the Green Door who hadn't been around during that terrible conflict. They wanted to know what had so suddenly chilled all the older, bitterly remembering men. The drunk Texan told them.

" That was in '62 boys, you recollect? The war run on for another three years. More'n a hundred thousand men died between '62 and '65."

The Texan wiped his eyes again, his humour entirely gone now. He twisted and flagged for another drink. He sagged over there against the bar and solemnly met all those still, rock-steady eyes which were lifted to him in the total silence of the room. He gently inclined his head.

" It's the truth, boys. There was twenty of us, all that was left of one company after the fightin', who were *there*—who saw it happen. Who saw the letter with Abe Lincoln's signature on it."

From a far corner table a man asked : " Why?"

The cowboy shrugged, tossed off his whisky and made a face, pushed the glass away and gazed steadily over where that inquiry had come from. " Why, mister? Well, I reckon unless you knew the man you'd rightly enough wonder why. I knew him. Knew him well twenty years back. He was a big, handsome feller with a way to him that captivated folks. He could smile into the maw of a cannon. He could ride any horse that was ever dropped and he could shoot as good with one hand as with the other. He was a gifted man—and he knew what he wanted from this lousy, stinkin' life, boys. Power. He came out of the cane-break swamps along the Rio Grande with his ribs showin' through from a diet of mealy cornpone and sow-bosom. An' he had a fire burnin' in him against poverty in any shape. He seen the fightin' comin', boys. He bought up barrels of salt-pork and he bought up good horses. Don't ask me how he wangled the money, all I can tell you is that he done got it somewhere. An' when the shootin' commenced there he was with the kind of stuff armies got to have. He made a lot of money, boys, which he put right back into more supplies." The cowboy made a ghastly grey grin. " Pretty picture, isn't it?" He asked, and not a soul in that room answered him.

" He didn't want no truce, boys, he wanted that rotten war to go on an' on."

" It did," mumbled a bull-bass-voiced, thickly set-up freighter with a stump where his left hand should have been. " It went on, Texas. It lacked four days of lastin' four damned years."

" Didn't it though," said the cowboy, gazing at that stump. " Yank; you're not the only one who lost a piece of himself." The cowboy looked around over the heads of his stationary audience. " A man lies under the stars many a night in my trade," he said, " an' he wonders a lot about things, an' he comes to some pretty sorry conclusions. Like—what kind of a man is it that doesn't care for anythin' in this world but money an' power? What makes a man like that? Why, if there's really a

God up there in His heaven, does he allow such people to go on livin'?"

Down the bar a bearded miner in a soiled old plaid shirt struck the bar with his fist and snarled at the aproned attendant. "Double shot," he commanded. "And set another one up for Johnny Reb down there." Then this hawk-faced older man turned upon big booted feet and said to the Texas cowboy, "You seen this old comrade of yours right here in Virginia City, Johnny Reb?"

"I have, pardner, like I told you before, in a shiny white shirt wearin' doeskin gloves and polished black boots." The Texan accepted his free drink, raised it to the rock-faced miner with one of those little, old-fashioned slight bows from the waist, and tossed it off neat. He put the glass down, balled his fist and squeezed his eyes until the fire burnt past his throat, then leaned there wagging his head back and forth. He was getting steadily drunker.

"Name him, Johnny Reb," said the bearded miner quietly. "Tell us who this old comrade from Hood's Brigade is."

The Texan didn't seem to hear, he leaned over the bar looking somewhat sick and kept on gently wagging his head back and forth. The stillness stretched out to its maximum length. He stopped moving his head, raised himself with a physical effort, turned drunkenly and looked out over the room. "I got to get out of your town," he muttered. "Boys, I got to ride on out of here an' bed down where there's fresh air and clean stars. Name him? Sure, boys. Funny thing what the passage of time'll do for men, isn't? I see a heap of Yankee faces amongst you, an' twenty years ago I'd have done my damndest to kill the passel of you. But time's changed

all that, hasn't it? Johnny Reb an' Johnny Shiloh sittin'
here together after twenty years, finally figurin' somethin'
out; finally figurin' out it wasn't you'n me who was the
real enemy. Sure, boys, I'll name him for you—then I
got to ride on southward out of your town because the
air here sort of strangles me. His name is—*Dallas
Wayne*."

No one knew whatever became of that Texas cowboy.
He kept his word, got unsteadily astride his horse and
rode southwards out of the lives of all those men in
the Green Door Saloon, out of the recollection of the
town, but he'd left behind something men couldn't forget, something unhealthy and evil and grisly: the
thought of hundreds of thousands of dead men in grey
uniforms and also in blue uniforms, lying low in the
smoky haze after a thousand battles, brought to their
end because one man had kept a plea for a truce from
reaching its destination.

Oh; the war probably would have been fought anyway. All those dead conceivably would still have died.
But no one, not even the stoutest apologists for Dallas
Wayne ever denied that except for his murder of one
man, perhaps they *wouldn't* have died, but yes or no,
they should have had at least that one *chance*. The
whole nation should have had it.

2

A WINTER passed and a summer came, after that Texas rider passed through Virginia City. The quiet talk got frayed and endlessly explored. There was of course an inevitable conclusion among the substantial people of the locality: Who put any faith in the drunken ramblings of a stranger who had, admittedly, been tossing off whisky like it was water that day a year before in the Green Door Saloon? And the answer was as usual among that certain solid, coldly practical and coldly analytical substantial strata of Nevada society: No one; no one but fool, and equally as dissolute range-riders, freighters, and men of that kind who hung out in places like the Green Door.

The banker still fawned when big smiling Dallas Wayne came to town. The merchants still eagerly sought his business. Besides, the war was long over now. But there was another inevitable aftermath of such a grisly accusation: people remembered; whichever view they took, they nevertheless remembered. Even when they were welcoming Dallas Wayne into their homes and stores, they were remembering, for such is the poison caused by unsubstantiated gossip. They might believe or not believe, but they remembered; there was a cloud

in their eyes when they greeted Dallas Wayne and there
lingered a cloud in their thoughts as well.

Time of course ameliorates all things, but it never
entirely erases, and a man like Dallas Wayne could
live to be a hundred and ultimately go into his grave
full of honours and there would still be those who remembered.

Another sidelight of such tales about powerful men
is that, while all the lesser people know, the powerful
man is usually the last one to hear. No one, friend or
enemy, is ever quite willing to tell him to his face he
stands accused of probable mass murder, much as it lies
in the hearts of the vicious to do this, so Dallas felt a
slight coolness but as time passed he noticed it less and
even when he first felt it, he more or less correctly put
it down to envy. Every man whose rise to wealth and
power has been sudden and spectacular feels himself to
be a reproach to all other men; feels that their envy is
simply part of the price he cheerfully pays to trample
across their secret pride, their secret envy.

Finally, Dallas had his endless details to watch over,
which insulated him against that silent storm down in
Virginia City too. He had his ranch, his herds, his
endless problems and decisions. They were his life and
his world. He lived for them and by them because that's
the kind of a man he was; resourceful, bold, fierce in a
velvety way, a user of people, a manipulator of men.

That silent storm subsided gradually, until the following summer, it was down to a groundswell of reticent
public opinion. Everyone of course knew, but everyone
also had their own problems to deal with, so, as winter-
time faded out into soft, sensuous springtime, and later
on, turned into the fierce glare of Nevada summertime,
the raw edge had been blunted considerably.

Then it unexpectedly flared up again, and this time more violently than anyone could have foreseen. All because of a woman, too. In fact, all because of a woman who had hardly been out of her cradle more than a couple of years when Hood's wild Texans had met that Yankee army and vanquished it some eighteen or nineteen years earlier.

Her name was Burlette Francine Smith. Her father had been the owner of the big Smith ranch southeast of Virginia City. Originally old Burl Smith and his two brothers had founded that ranch, but the brothers had passed on; one had been found dead in his bed, the other had died when a runaway stagecoach had flung itself over a canyon wall. Old Burl, the last of the Smith men, had been standing by his corrals after a sweaty hot day of dust and blue-blazing profanity, the active ingredients of any worthwhile big cattle roundup, resting and catching his breath. He had been only fifty-four that day with a normal expectancy of at least— barring accidents—another ten years on earth. Ted Sloan his foreman had just ridden up to fling sweat off his chin and report the roundup a complete success when Burl Smith's eyes slowly widened. He lifted his right hand to squeeze at his chest; he hadn't uttered a blessed sound, he just jack-knifed forward and was dead from heart stoppage by the time he hit the ground.

So, Burlette had come home from the east where she'd been visiting, had dutifully buried old Burl, and had kept Ted Sloan on his foreman's job with a cool, efficient capability that awed most of her neighbours and acquaintances and which also, in a somewhat different manner, caused her to be the envy of all the other ranch-wives and daughters of that southerly Nevada world of cattle and heat and rough men on sleek horses.

She had of course heard of meteoric Dallas Wayne, and he, in turn, had known of her. Actually though, neither had ever seen the other except distantly or casually. But Dallas, with range-adjacencies, had known old Burl well enough. Like most self-sufficient men of wealth and substance, neither of them had ever sought the other's company, still and all, they'd known each other, and in their own, totally different ways they had gotten along well enough.

Burlette Francine was a grey-eyed slim, straight girl with an inquiring, direct look to her, a long, composed mouth and a temper that showed in the swift way she turned to answer a question or to ask one. There was something quietly assured about her, something masculine and straightforward which was the heritage of a girl raised by men. Her mother had died of galloping consumption many years back, so she'd matured under the steadying influence of her father and his two bachelor brothers. She accordingly rarely showed the frills, the coquetry, of girls, and on horseback she could actually be mistaken for a man, which was how Dallas Wayne got into trouble one early June morning with the blue-blurred prairie wearing its summertime haziness and with the big yellow sun flattening perspective and telescoping distances until a moving object in all that endlessness could be one mile away or five miles away.

She was riding with Ted Sloan to examine a band of loose horses the Smith ranch-hands had corralled three miles from her headquarters place, when Dallas and his rangeboss, Curly Winters, along with three of Dallas's Texas men, rode up at that same corral to sit stonily gazing in at some thirty or forty horses, mostly wearing the big DW brand on their hips.

She knew who Dallas was, of course, and although she

didn't know his foreman or his riders, Ted Sloan knew them all. Ted was part Indian; a small part, yet it showed in his black, straight hair, his black, yeasty eyes, and also in the habit he had of sitting for long periods of time looking and listing and saying very little, which is what he did when the two parties met near the old corrals where those horses were.

Dallas was courtly and Burlette was polite. There should have perhaps been no trouble at all. Certainly, one rancher corralling nuisance-horses running loose in large numbers on his range—or *her* range—was nothing unusual; nothing for anyone to get prickly about. And even though most of those animals weren't branded it still shouldn't have been any insurmountable problem. Usually, when something like a question of ownership arose under these circumstances, the owner of the branded animals claimed his marked horses, then the unbranded beasts were equally divided, and that was that. Particularly, when the principals were both wealthy people with more than enough of their own marked horses, there was no cause for trouble.

But trouble, particularly after a long dry hot period, seemed always to be lurking close to the surface in men like Ted Sloan who'd heard that grisly story about Dallas Wayne, and also in Curly Winters, who'd always scorned 'breed Indians because, as a native Southwesterner, he'd come to manhood disliking Indians generally, full-bloods or half-bloods. And Curly was a Texan. So were the men with him Texans. Texans just naturally looked on Indians as something to be carefully watched, and killed at the first wrong move.

But Sloan didn't make the first wrong move, Dallas did, and he didn't perhaps actually mean to, either. All he said was, considering the strong, pleasant contours

of Burlette Smith's features, "Eleven horses in there belong to me. The balance are probably at least half mine,
but you're welcome to them, Miss Smith. The reason I
rode over was because I heard your men had corralled
them where there was no water."

It was true; there was no way for those tucked-up
animals to get a drink and the temperature out there
upon the shadeless range was over a hundred degrees. It
was, in the minds of Dallas Wayne, his rangeboss and
his Texas riders, a callous, needlessly cruel thing to do
to dumb horse-brutes. It was very easy for those Texas
minds, also, to equate that kind of senseless brutality
with an Indian, a part Indian, or a just plain cruel
person male or female.

Ted Sloan's black gaze lifted to Dallas Wayne's face
and lingered there. He'd caught that undercurrent of
Texas thought all right. But Ted said nothing and
Burlette, letting Wayne's innuendo go past, said, "This
time of year, Mister Wayne, Circle S needs all its grass.
Free-running loose-stock is corralled by my men at my
orders."

"Without water?" asked Curly Winters.

That was the spark that caused the flame.

"They got water over on DW range," said Ted
Sloan, suddenly reacting to Curly's cold look at Burlette
Smith. "If you'd keep 'em where they belong we
wouldn't have to spend good time runnin' 'em down."

Dallas shifted his glance, dropped it upon the 'breed
foreman of Circle S and considered Sloan a trifle flintily.
"They'll live," he said in that quiet Texas voice of his.
"No harm's been done, Sloan. Just turn 'em out and
we'll take back the branded ones." Then Dallas looked
back at Burlette. "There is also water over here on
Circle S," he said, perhaps unintentionally, perhaps in-

tentionally, backing up his foreman's observation. " If
it happens again maybe you folks could corral 'em where
they wouldn't suffer."

" We corral strays, Mister Wayne, wherever it's handy
to do so," said Burlette. " I run a cow ranch, not a home
for foundling horses which have been—perhaps—deliberately drifted over onto my grass."

Now, the words had been said, the looks exchanged,
which could not be taken back, and as ridiculous as
the cause may have been, it was not one bit less ridiculous
than dozens of other causes which had soaked cow-
country range in the blood of fiercely partisan, fiercely
violent, men.

Dallas coloured a little. His long-lipped mouth drew
out thin. Beside him Curly Winters regarded Burlette
Smith as he might have considered a cow-killing she-
cougar; with quick, flashing resentment and veiled but
very strong disapproval. The other Texans too, showed
venom in their looks, but they were less interested in their
employer and in Sloan's employer; they curled their
scornful lips at a 'breed, content to settle for an enemy
on their level, if in fact he turned into an enemy, otherwise they were satisfied just to show contempt, to show
Texas scorn for a mixed-blood redman.

Dallas said softly and stiffly, " Ma'am, I don't have to
trespass on anyone's grass, least of all yours. I could put
your Circle S in a corner of my most worthless range
and still have more than enough left over. And ma'am,
one more thing : your paw and your uncles, when they
were alive, got along fine with DW. It's a right good
policy, Miss Burlette. A right good policy." Dallas looked
around. " Curly, open the corral, cut out the branded
horses and let's get back."

But Burlette Francine hadn't quite finished yet. " Take

them all," she said to Dallas, and also turned her head away from the Texans to say, " Ted; let them out and head them for DW range. We don't need any horses we aren't positive belong to us."

Curly and his companions were already riding towards that corral gate when Burlette Francine gave her order. But Ted Sloan was closer, so when he reined away to obey, those five men mixed together at the gate. Someone growled something, the fierce, evil yellow sunlight burnt steadily downward, a man swore with quick, breathless anger and someone swung with a gloved fist. Ted Sloan, struck across the back of the head just below his hat, crumpled and fell to the ground under the fidgeting shod hooves of DW horses.

" Here," said Curly Winters sharply, peering down at Sloan. " What the hell!"

It had happened without any great haste and yet Winters hadn't been quite prepared for it, so there he sat, hauling back on the reins to keep his horse from stepping upon the Circle S foreman. The other Texans also hauled back. No one seemed to understand which man, in a surge of hot fury, had struck Sloan down.

Burlette moved too, but not as quickly as big Dallas Wayne did. He spun his horse and crackled an order which made his cowboys draw off still further. Then he stepped down, stepped up, and as Sloan sat up, blinked and streaked for his holstered .45, Dallas aimed a kick with one pointed-toed boot.

They all heard the sickening crunch of breaking wristbones.

Sloan went over sideways, threw out his oddly hanging right hand to catch himself, and the grinding bone-ends failed to support him. He fell heavily into the churned earth.

Burlette left her saddle and started ahead. Dallas set his back to her, caught Sloan by the shoulder and heaved him roughly to his feet. Curly Winters hit the ground and set himself squarely facing Burlette; now, his former look of uncertain disapproval was no longer so uncertain. Curly was a Texan; he knew all the ancient patterns of this kind of violence, and if he'd never before fought a woman, he nevertheless knew how to.

Sloan tore clear of Dallas's grip, his eyes black with glazed malice and anguish. He started to bend down for his gun where it lay but Dallas was quicker, he placed one big foot over the weapon and tipped up his considerable weight.

"You're a fool," he told Circle S's foreman. "Don't ever try drawing on me again. Now get on your horses —both of you—and ride off."

There was nothing left for Ted Sloan and Burlette Smith to do. For the Circle S foreman death was waiting in five different holsters. For the handsome girl who was now white to the eyes, there was the bitterest of all sensations—defeat at the hands of this man she'd heard a terrible story about, on her own land, at her own corrals.

3

THAT WAS the beginning of the long, hot summer for Dallas Wayne, and yet no retaliation came at once. He had two herds to put together, one for the Piute Reservation contract he had, the other, long three-year-old steers, to be pushed over to rails-end for shipment east, and because there were close to a thousand head involved in each of these gathers, Dallas was kept busy for over a week.

But he eventually got down to Virginia City where there was a little unpleasantness with a man named Brannan over a a logging operation. Dallas owned the land where Brannan was felling his timber for milling and shipment to San Francisco. Brannan had gone beyond the limits of Dallas's land to get more choice sawlogs, and because the owner of that land who had been trespassed upon bitterly complained, George Stubblefield, the banker in town, had sent a note to Dallas urging him to come into Virginia City and straighten the mess out.

Dallas had come. It was a hot afternoon by the time he rode on in and left his horse at the liverybarn. There were a number of other local cowmen in town, some gravely nodded as Dallas swung past and some turned their backs upon him so that they would not have to acknowledge his presence; these were the men who'd heard of Ted Sloan's broken right wrist and how he got it, and hadn't yet made up their minds whether to condemn Wayne or Circle S. Until they made up their minds they'd ignore both sides.

Of course everyone else in Virginia City had heard of that encounter also, and while there had been nothing premeditated about what had happened at Circle S's corrals, people said there had been; said that if Wayne hadn't meant to make trouble he wouldn't have brought Curly Winters and three more men with him.

They also said, the ones who were willing to believe the worst of Dallas Wayne, and it had its mote of truth : just what right had *he* to invade Circle S land and provoke a fight!

George Stubblefield in his gloomy office at the *Virginia City Stockmen's Bank*, had heard just about everything which had been said about the Sloan Affair, but George was a discreet man. He wouldn't say a word if it were left to him to make that decision.

Stubblefield was a short, nondescript man with sandy hair, little blue eyes, lips set in an expression of scepticism, and a philosophy which had recently been expanded—after that grisly rumour concerning Dallas Wayne during the war—to include anyone as being thoroughly acceptable so long as they didn't get arrested, and so long as they kept a healthy account at his bank.

When Dallas walked in Stubblefield quickly brought him a chair. When Dallas blew out a ragged breath and commented upon the heat, Stubblefield was there with a commiserating little series of understanding clucking sounds. Then, when Dallas asked about the logging operation, Stubblefield had placed the tips of the fingers of one hand against the tips of the fingers of his other hand, and had dryly and precisely explained exactly what had occurred. Then he said, " But getting damages from Brannan won't be possible, Dallas. You see, he pulled out lock, stock, and barrel, three days ago, which, if you'll recall, is the same day I sent you the note to come into town about this matter."

Dallas wasn't troubled—not yet. If he had to pay the damages himself he'd survive; besides, Brannan had paid him in advance for logging off Dallas's land, so he'd made his comfortable profit. He sprawled there in George Stubblefield's office dwarfing the other, older man. His legs were thrust out their full and considerable length, his hands hung from heavy wrists over the sides of the chair, and curtained-off windows to keep out the heat made Dallas's bronzed, rich colouring much darker, all but his light eyes and his big strong, white teeth when he spoke.

" In other words," he said, " I'm hooked for the damages. Is that it, George?"

" That's it, I'm afraid. Now, if you'd come in the day I—"

" Couldn't. Had two big drives to get under way."

" Well; it'd probably have saved you money. At least you'd have been able to stop Brannan before he pulled out."

Dallas nodded. Why was it that always being right was so terribly important to people like Stubblefield? " What will these trespass-damages amount to, George?"

Stubblefield's finger pads pressed tighter, his little blue eyes swung away and swung back. He took back a big breath. " Ten thousand dollars, Dallas."

For a long moment Dallas Wayne sat there too dumbfounded to speak, his angular, flat, tough body still all loose and easy in the chair. Then he began to slowly gather himself together. Slow-rising dark blood rose up from his throat into his cheeks.

"George," he drawled, his voice very soft now, very gentle-sounding, "you're joking."

Stubblefield lowered his hands, fished for a limp handkerchief and wiped sweat off his palms. He didn't like this; he knew these Texans and he didn't like the way big Dallas Wayne was looking at him now. Didn't like it at all.

"Let me explain," he said, forcing up a grey look of partisan affability. "Brannan logged off about a hundred acres, Dallas, of some very prime—"

"George," broke in Dallas, sitting straight up in his chair now and steadily considering the banker. "Get to the point. You know as well as I do there's hardly ten thousand dollars worth of saw logs in this whole damned countryside. What's this about; does someone think they're going to hold me up?"

"Maybe that Sloan affair out at—"

"Sloan? Ted Sloan? What the devil's that got to do with this, George?"

"Dallas; those trees and that acreage belong to Circle S."

Again big Dallas Wayne just sat there staring across at banker Stubblefield. Understanding came slowly but it came. *She* was doing this. It was preposterous. Even if they went to court, there wasn't a judge in the territory who'd give her those kind of damages for a hundred or so acres of trees. It was ridiculous. He snorted and struck the arms of his chair with both big, work-roughened hands. "Women," he said, and swore loudly enough for his swords to slam back and forth between the office walls. "This doesn't even make sense."

"Well," Stubblefield put in uneasily, "as I said before,

it's probably because of that Sloan thing, Dallas. She's a lot like her father was."

" I don't give a damn who she's like," rapped out Wayne, then he abruptly closed his lips, put his head a little to one side and fixed a cruel gaze upon the banker. " George; whose side are you on; what's your interest in this?"

Stubblefield spread his hands out, palms up. He'd long since anticipated that question and he'd long since formulated his answer to it. Dallas Wayne was a big depositor but so was the Circle S ranch. He had no wish to lose either of those accounts. In fact, he didn't mean to lose them, so he said, " She hired an attorney, Dallas, and she sent him down here to me."

" Yeah? Why didn't she send him to me, George?"

" Well; I reckon she didn't want him to go out to your place because there might be more trouble."

Dallas shook his head over this. " No. She *wants* trouble with me. If she'd thought I'd rough up her lawyer she'd have deliberately sent him to the ranch."

Stubblefield shrugged. He'd successfully sidestepped that paramount issue which had formerly bothered him a little—the matter of losing Dallas Wayne's account— so he now relaxed a little and said, " Who knows how a woman's mind works? All I know is that she sent her attorney to me and I said I'd talk to you."

" She's going to sue me?"

Stubblefield gravely inclined his head. " Ten thousand dollars worth. Now, what I've got in mind is for you to see her, talk to her, Dallas. Those damages shouldn't be more than three to five hundred dollars. I drove out there yesterday with a friend of mine who knows timber. He says five hundred would be tops for the trees Brannan took."

" Brannan," growled big Dallas Wayne. " I'd like to get my hands on him for ten minutes."

" By now, with his three days start, he'll be somewhere along the Humboldt on his way to San Francisco. I don't think you could catch him."

Dallas stood up. " I don't mean to catch him. Damn that woman anyway."

" If you rode over there and maybe talked to her."

" *Talked* to her! Is that her idea, George, or her lawyer's idea?"

" No. It's my idea, Dallas. Listen; I serve you both. I'm a friend to you both. What I *don't* want to see is trouble between you and Circle S. Now that meeting at her corrals where Ted Sloan got hurt . . ."

" He tried to draw on me, George. I kicked the gun out of his hand. I didn't mean to break his wrist, I only meant to keep from getting shot by the damned 'breed."

" I know. We've all heard how that happened."

" All? What do you mean—all?"

" Here in town and out on the range too, I reckon. Things like that spread around fast. You know how that is. People talk, they carry tales, they gossip." Stubblefield was watching Wayne's face closely. There was that other much more grisly bit of gossip too, that people knew about. He was seeking some inkling that Wayne might also have heard of this. But Wayne evidently hadn't because when next he spoke it was with all his attention upon this other matter.

He said : " Going over to talk to her wouldn't change anything, George. I don't know exactly how that trouble started over at her corrals, but I *do* know that she was primed for it. The way she looked at me—at my men. The things she said an' the way she said them. She was ready for trouble."

" Well," said the banker, finally standing up over behind his desk, "but that's not the direct issue here,
Dallas. If you two go to court there's going to be trouble.
Not just in court but anywhere your DW riders meet
her Circle S men. It could even spread to the community,
to the ranges. This has been a hot, dry summer; people's
nerves are raw-edged. And Dallas, one more thing:
who'll win? I'll tell you—no one. The lawyers will ride
off with her money and with your money. They'll be the
only ones who'll benefit. Now please, make some effort
to talk to her."

Wayne lifted his darkly troubled face. "Have you
talked like this to *her*?" he drawled.

Stubblefield shook his head.

"Then send *her* a note too, George. Get her in your
office like you've done with me. Give her the same
arguments. I'll pay any reasonable damages. And George
—one more thing—if her lawyer tries to keep this thing
boiling so's he'll be sure of his fee, you take him off to
one side and tell him I'll guarantee him his money if
there's no lawsuit, but if he pushes for a court trial . . ."
Dallas lifted big shoulders and dropped them, his cruel
meaning clear enough. " You tell him that, too."

Stubblefield's uneasiness began to return. Dallas was
manoeuvring him into the middle and actually all he'd
ever meant to do was advise, to placate, to manipulate
the principals, because, banker-like, he loved to play
God. But what was happening was that Dallas Wayne
was doing the manipulating; was jockeying Stubblefield squarely into the thankless and perilous role of
mediator.

" I don't know, Dallas," he uncomfortably murmured.
" This really is beyond the scope of my duties here at
the bank."

" You called me in, didn't you? Is my account insignificant to you, George?"

" No, of course not, Dallas. Your account's one of the largest we have."

" And you want to keep it, George?"

Stubblefield fumbled for the initiative he'd subtly lost and failed now to regain. He screwed up his face into an expression of pain. He tried to skirt around this issue. " But really, it seems to me you and Burlette, and I reckon that attorney of hers too, are the ones to—"

" George," said Dallas Wayne blandly as he stepped back towards the office door, " Do as much for her as you've done for me. I'm obliged to you an' if she's got anything besides ice in her veins she will be too. And let me know the outcome after you've seen her. Now I've got to get back and finish the contract paperwork on my reservation beef contract so's I'll get paid." Dallas squeezed the door latch and amiably smiled at Stubblefield. " As soon as I get that government voucher I'll fetch it down for deposit."

Stubblefield weakly smiled. Those federal vouchers were for a lot of money. He knew exactly why Wayne had said that too; Stubblefield had been used. Dallas Wayne had passed the entire mess right back to him again; had manoeuvred him squarely into the middle of his fight with Circle S. As Wayne left the office Stubblefield sank back into his chair with a bad feeling; with a premonition that, although he was an excellent banker, he was nowhere near the match of Dallas Wayne in the kind of trouble he feared now was about to flame up between the two biggest cow outfits in the area.

But Stubblefield also had another worry. He knew as surely as he knew his own name that in any fight with Dallas Wayne, Burl Smith's girl was going to lose.

Whether she used lawyers or gunmen or her own feminine wiles, she was going to lose, and that meant, to banker Stubblefield, that Dallas Wayne would very probably wind up owning Circle S too. If *that* happened, George Stubblefield would also lose. Burl Smith and his brothers had helped found Stubblefield's bank. They'd left their stock to Burlette. Wayne would end up with that stock as sure as God made green apples, and of all the people in Virginia City or its environs whom George Stubblefield *didn't* want over him as majority stockholder, Dallas Wayne was foremost. The reason? Exactly what had occurred just now in his office; George wanted to be the lord of his little domain; *he* wanted to do the manipulating. With big Dallas Wayne he'd be overshadowed, would be always and everlastingly outthought, out-manoeuvred, and ground down to face up to the wretched fact that he was and always had been, nothing but a little man.

An anxious, worried little man could be dangerous.

4

DALLAS WAYNE didn't forget his visit with George Stubblefield; how could he? Ten thousand dollars was a fortune. But when he got back to the ranch Curly was waiting. There was a man over at the house waiting to see Dallas, Curly reported. Then he said as though they were conspirators: " I want to tell you somethin', Dallas. Maybe this feller's here to make trouble an' maybe he ain't, but the boys an' me've talked it over an' if you say the word we'll just sort of ease him off the place."

Dallas considered his fair, lanky rangeboss and smiled. This was a warming experience. He shook his head though, handed Curly the reins to his horse, started across to the long, low adobe house, and pushed all thought of Stubblefield and Burlette Smith into the far back of his mind. Not for a long time did he think of those two again.

But the stranger was no one to fear. His name was Cavendish and he'd been sent down by the Indian Agent to inspect the cattle which were being held out on the range for the northward drive to the Piute Reservation. He had his buggy handy so he and Dallas drove on out to look over the herd.

The moment Cavendish drove up out there where

Dallas's Texans had their holding-ground camp, though,
Dallas noticed something : his men eyed Cavendish coldly
and made a particular point of keeping aloof from the
stranger, something he'd never had happen before. This
puzzled him a little. He thought back to Curly's words
and attributed this attitude to Curly's remarks, and yet
there occurred to him no real reason for such an attitude.
His men were a little on edge expecting some retaliation
from Circle S over the Ted Sloan affair, but obviously
the Indian Agent's man wasn't likely to be at all involved in that purely local matter, so Dallas's perplexity
remained all the while he and Cavendish were driving
around and through the gather. Finally, when Cavendish
was satisfied with the quality of the beef and turned back
towards the ranch, Dallas asked him to halt a moment.
He left Cavendish, walked over to the little camp, eyed
his riders and selected one, a rough, older man named
Frank Webster, and took Frank off a little distance.

"What's the trouble out here?" he inquired, and
Webster kept watching Cavendish down there in his top-
buggy as he answered.

"We been scouted twice this mornin', and once it was
by a feller in a rig like that, boss."

Dallas gazed at Webster. Scouted? On his own range
someone had spied on his men at the gathering-ground?
It didn't make sense. It didn't make sense particularly
that anyone would sneak around on DW range in a
top-buggy; any horseman, if he felt the urge to do so,
could run down a buggy.

"You sure it was a top-buggy like that one?" he
asked, and Webster nodded grimly, his pale eyes and
battered, rugged features, pinched down with suspicion
and antagonism.

"Same kind of an outfit, boss," he muttered. "An' we

been talkin' about it. We figure it's Circle S up to something. They've had time enough to do whatever they figure to do about Ted Sloan."

" Hell," growled Dallas. " Not in a top-buggy, Frank." Then a sudden thought struck him. A Circle S man wouldn't show up on DW range in a top-buggy—but a Circle S *woman* might. " Frank; you boys sort of fan out an' look around. As soon as I get back to the ranch I'll grab a fresh animal and join you out here. If that rig's still on DW land we'll run it down."

" Boss; that rig wasn't alone. The first time it snuck up there was riders with it. Looked like maybe three, four men."

" All right, Frank. I'll fetch back Curly and the other men."

Webster nodded, looked grimly pleased at the prospect of striking back at this obvious spy, and stalked on back to the cow-camp.

Dallas said very little all the way back to the ranch. As soon as he decently could he got rid of Cavendish, called for Curly Winters to saddle him a fresh animal, went into the house to take down a carbine from the parlour wall-rack then hastened on down to the barn where Curly was waiting, not with one saddled animal but with two.

" Better round up whoever you've got here at the home-place too," he told Winters, then explained about the mysterious snoopers out by the gathering-ground. Curly listened, nodded, looked off northwesterly in the direction of Circle S and said he'd already sent the rest of the riding crew on ahead to help hold the gather.

Dallas led the way back. It wasn't a long ride. He and Curly got back out there in something over an hour. Frank Webster wasn't around but another cowboy was, and this one said he'd been detailed to watch things at the camp, that everyone else was out hunting up those strangers. He then gestured off due west and said that was the direction he'd last seen the riders and the top-buggy.

Curly and Dallas loped out. The whole thing puzzled Curly considerably. " But why'n hell," he wanted to know, " would anyone do such a lousy job of spyin'? If I wanted to know what the boys was doin' out here, danged if I'd let 'em see me spyin' on them."

Dallas had no ready answer for that, and in fact he wouldn't have gotten an opportunity to expound it if he'd had one, because two riders came whipping towards him from the southwest, riding close together and moving swiftly along. One of these men was recognisable as they got closer as Frank Webster. At sight of Curly and Dallas Wayne, Frank veered to intercept them. He slowed a hundred yards out, slackened off with his reins and came ahead the last little intervening distance at a slogging walk, and he said without any preliminary greetings to either the rangeboss or to Dallas, " Well, we got 'em. One got away, but I don't figure he even knew we was after 'em. Boss?"

" Yes."

" It was Miss Burlette Smith in that rig. Them three men with her are Circle S hands. The one who left 'em an' run on ahead, was Ted Sloan."

Dallas considered Webster's bitter expression. The rider who'd come up with Webster had been one of those men over at the corrals when Sloan had been knocked off his horse. This man, a long-faced, lantern-jawed Texan, drawlingly said, " Boss; she's madder'n a hornet. So are them fellers with her."

Winters, who knew these rangeriders better than

Dallas did because he shared their everyday existence with them, now said, " You boys got her out there somewhere; 'you holdin' her?"

Webster swivelled his testy eyes to Winters and nodded. " The boss said we was to sort of scout around for 'em, an' we did." He lifted his rein-hand. " Come on; we'll take you out there."

Dallas almost demurred about this, but as Webster, Winters and the lantern-jawed rider spun their horses, Dallas shrugged and loped out with them. It didn't make any sense at all to him, what Burlette Smith was doing. The longer he loped along with his men the less sense it made to him.

If the handsome girl hadn't known any better than to allow herself to be caught at something as foolish as sneaking around on someone else's range—in a top-buggy, of all things—then, Sloan should have, because he was a born-and-bred rangeman.

"Yonder," growled Frank Webster, raising a thick arm to point off in the heat-hazed middle distance where a drowsing harness-horse stood drooping between the shafts of a top-buggy, and several men stood awkwardly around, waiting.

Dallas closed the last half mile with a vertical line between his brows. This faint, perplexed look didn't leave even after he rode up, halted, and sat there gazing downward.

Burlette was in buggy-shade among her three men. She returned Dallas Wayne's look as coolly as though this meeting held no significance to her at all. The Circle S men with her were flinty, hard-eyed men. They hadn't been disarmed but twenty feet away four DW riders were watching them with their whole, roiled-up attention.

Dallas stepped down, moved up to his horse's head and gazed straight down into the handsome girl's tawny grey eyes. " Mind explaining what you were doing over here on DW range?" he said.

Her answer was quick and brief. " Looking for strays. Did I break a law, Mister Wayne?"

Dallas reached up to ease his hat back. He didn't answer; he looked at each Circle S man individually. This wasn't right; it didn't look right and it didn't feel right. " Where's Sloan?" he asked.

None of the Circle S riders said a thing, and even Burlette was slow in replying, but when she ultimately did her voice was still frostily cool and succinct towards him.

" He's not here. But what difference does that make?"

" None," conceded Dallas, lowering his eyes to her face. " Do you always go looking for strays using a top-buggy, Miss Smith?"

" When I feel like it, Mister Wayne. Shouldn't I?"

" Should you?" he countered, turning just a little annoyed.

" Why yes I should, Mister Wayne—if I want to be seen."

Curly and Frank Webster both scratched their heads at the same time while gazing steadily at Burlette Smith, and neither of them was aware that the other was also doing this. The other DW men were becoming increasingly puzzled too. It showed in their expressions and also in the way they kept warily watching those three Circle S men.

Somewhere, a considerable distance off, someone fired a gun. Just for a second, so deep was the DW perplexity, that this flat, faint sound went unheeded. Then Curly

Winters swung violently around, and one second behind him, Frank Webster also violently reacted.

There were two more shots, a long pause, then a final solitary shot. The Circle S men seemed suddenly very tense. They watched the DW men, especially Curly and Frank Webster. They also watched Dallas Wayne, but he hadn't turned at the sound of those shots; hadn't in fact so much as moved a muscle. He stood there staring straight down at Burlette Smith, and she gave him back stare for stare.

Winters ripped out a mild oath and lunged for his horse. Dallas halted him with two words: " Hold it." He then lifted his head slightly, gazed with a sudden very cold detachment at the Circle S men and said, " Shuck your guns, boys."

The Circle S men didn't obey.

Dallas lifted his lip in a slow, tough smile. " All right, boys, don't shuck 'em." He dropped his right hand straight down. *" Draw them!"*

No one doubted from the expression on big Dallas Wayne's face that this time when a Circle S man fell, it would be no accidental or impromptu thing.

Burlette said over her shoulder. " Do as he says. Shed your guns. This is his range. He has the right."

The guns were dropped.

Curly, beside his horse, stepped away. So did Frank Webster. The other DW riders alternated between looking back behind them and looking straight ahead at their prisoners. Clearly, they were more troubled now than puzzled. They remained that way for only a moment longer, for when Dallas spoke once more to Burlette Smith, he cleared up the mystery of those distant gunshots with a bull's-eye-guess.

" Is this how you fight?" he asked, his gaze cold. " You

wanted my men to see you in the buggy. You wanted them to come out to investigate. Isn't that it?"

Those wintry grey eyes never waved as Burlette answered right back. " That's it exactly, Mister Wayne. But the fighting part of it isn't correct. *You* declared this war, Circle S didn't."

" So you've just now stampeded my gather out there. You've sent Sloan and the balance of your crew out around and down where there's only one DW man on guard, to stampede the weight off those Reservation cattle."

" There's no water at your holding-ground, Mister Wayne. We thought, since you're so sensitive about animals having access to water—"

" If you were a man I'd kill you," Dallas broke in to softly say. " As it is, I've got a notion to take my belt to you."

Curly Winters was standing as stiff as a ramrod, staring. So was Frank Webster. To the DW riders it all dawned very slowly how this had been planned and successfully executed. It appalled them. Not that they'd been taken in by that fake scouting-up of their campground which aroused their suspicions and drew them off so the herd could be hit and scattered, but that this quite lovely, smoky-eyed woman was capable of doing such a thing.

Then Burlette Smith said something that made those tough Texans gasp, for every one of them had also heard that old rumour about their employer, but had rarely spoken of it even among themselves.

She said, " Take your belt to a woman, Mister Wayne? I understood your method of handling defenceless people was to—cut their throats. Or don't you have your Bowie knife with you today?"

Dallas Wayne's external aplomb faded. His face whitened to the hairline and his eyes became pieces of glazed ice. " What d'you mean by that?" he whispered.

But she turned, set her back to him, stepped up into her top-buggy and reached down for the looped lines. She undoubtedly would have driven away, but big Dallas Wayne brushed those three men of hers aside as thought they were insignificant obstacles, caught the lines and held them in one big fist.

" I asked you a question," he said, using that same very quiet, very deadly drawl of his. " What did you mean by that remark you just made—ma'am?"

She turned only her head. They were very close. Her riders as well as his, seemed to have forgotten everything but this slow, intense confrontation, and if any of those men ever afterwards recalled any of this vividly, it was the way she didn't drop her eyes nor even blink, in the face of his very lethal glare.

" I meant, *Mister* Wayne, that slashing the throat of an unarmed Union agent near Sabine Pass during the war, marked you for the kind of a man you were then— and still are—to the people of Nevada Territory. A bully and a murderer!"

She wrenched free the lines, flicked them, and drove off leaving him standing there as though he'd been suddenly turned to stone.

5

IT REQUIRED two full days to get those reservation cattle gathered again and the Texans went about it saying very little but with their expressions set and tough. Curly took the whole crew out to help at this because there was a definite deadline to the delivery-date. When he and some of the men came together at their little dry-camp that second evening to share coffee and beans before the extra-gang went back to the home place, Frank Webster said what was strongly in his mind as he flung off his saddle and turned his horse loose.

" Curly; why don't he just burst her wide open like a rotten melon? Why does he take this from her?"

Winters sipped the scalding brew and held the cup down to blow on it. " How would I know? Maybe because she's a female. I haven't seen him since yesterday anyway. He went to town."

That lantern-jawed cowboy drawled caustically that, female or not, Dallas should have given her a taste of his belt. Then this man offered his own philosophy about women in general and Burlette Smith in particular, saying, " Three things in this life I purely can't abide, bitin' dogs, kickin' horses an' female women with sharp tongues."

But it was the youthful cowboy who'd been the only one at their camp when Sloan had hit the herd shooting his gun and yelling, that brought things back into focus. " So now he knows," this one muttered, poking at their little brushfire. " Sooner or later'd he'd undoubtedly have heard that gossip anyway."

They all understood what the young rider meant and became thoughtfully pensive over their coffee cups. It was evening but the soft after-glow of hot daylight still lingered. The sun was gone though, so it was a little cooler. It was, in fact, a good time of day to sit and visit a little, and since Curly was in no big rush to get back the extra-gang sat on too.

One of those extra men said sombrely, " You're right, kid, he'd have heard it sooner or later. What's been stickin' in my craw was his reaction when he finally did hear it." This man looked across the fire at Winters. " How about it, Curly; how'd he act on the way back after we set them Circle S boys loose?"

" Like a big hunk of granite," answered Curly, testing the coffee to determine whether blowing upon it had made it cool enough to drink yet. It hadn't so he lowered the cup. " Didn't say two words all the way back. Just rode along like a feller who'd been kicked in the guts by a—"

" You reckon he knew what she meant?"

" He knew."

The young cowboy was trying to catch a struggling insect, which had dived into his coffee, using a thin twig. He said, " Then he sure-enough knew what she meant, an' I'd guess maybe—"

Frank Webster, realising what the youngest of them was about to say, interrupted with a hard growl, " I don't believe that. Didn't believe it when I first heard it.

I been around a little longer'n most of you fellers an' let me tell you somethin'—when a man's that rotten it comes out. I've been workin' for Dallas Wayne three years now. I've seen him mad an' worried and anxious— an' I've never seen no real, gen-u-wine meanness come out. Nossir; I don't believe he cut that Yankee's gullet like folks say, an' furthermore I'd like to meet the feller who started that talk."

Curly Winters put aside the cup of coffee, stood up and beat dust off his britches. He jerked his head at the extra-gang and they also arose. Webster and his companions would stay with the gather until Dallas picked the men who would start trailing it northward.

Curly said, " Frank; until she said that he hadn't heard the gossip, I'd bet money on that."

" Sure," Webster agreed. " A feller could see that from the shocked look on his face."

" Frank . . . how come him to know exactly what she was talkin' about, then?"

Winters and Webster exchanged a long look before Curly turned and led the extra-gang on over to their saddled horses. Even after Winters and his companions were riding off Frank Webster kept gazing after them. He too, had just been shocked.

The men with Curly Winters poked along southward without saying very much. The light began to fail, finally, and a rash of weak-lighted stars showed across the under-sides of heaven. There was a strong smell of cattle in the breathless air. They passed the bed-ground where that other herd had been briefly held for the final tally before being sent over to rails-end with six riders Dallas had hired on temporarily expressly for that purpose.

When they came within sight of the ranch buildings there was no light showing from the main house so someone made the obvious comment that Dallas hadn't returned from town yet. They were a half mile closer when Curly made out the shadowy silhouette of a top-buggy over in front of the barn. He had seen his share of those rigs in the last day or two and viewed this one suspiciously as he led the extra-gang on into the yard, growled for them to put up the horses, go start the supper fire in the bunkhouse, while he had a look around.

It was a short look. George Stubblefield was sitting in a rocking chair upon the broad veranda; he'd seen the extra-gang return and was waiting. As Curly stepped up onto the porch Stubblefield gravely nodded and said, " I've been waiting for Dallas. Is he with you?"

Winters shook his head. He knew who Stubblefield was but that was about the extent of their acquaintanceship. " If you came from town you should've seen him," said Curly. " He left the ranch early this morning."

" For Virginia City?"

" Well; he didn't tell me, but I figured that was where he was heading."

Stubblefield pursed his lips. " Odd; I didn't see him and I didn't leave town until after noon."

Curly didn't think it was odd. He dryly said, " You ever go to the Green Door?" And the way Stubblefield made a little sniffing look told Curly all he had to know. " On your way back look in there," he said. " That is, if findin' him's that important to you."

Stubblefield squared around in his chair and gazed around the big, prosperous-looking ranch yard. There was a glow of steady orange light coming from the big bunkhouse now, and down at the barn two men, obviously forking feed to the corralled and stalled animals, flutingly called back and forth to one another in the quiet, soft gloom of late evening.

"Fine big ranch," the banker murmured.

"Took work to make it that," said Curly bluntly, resenting just a little bit the way Stubblefield was sitting possessively there. "Takes more work to keep it like that."

"Yes," mused Stubblefield. "Tell me something; has Dallas gotten his drives off yet?"

"The one to rails-end is gone, but the reservation gather's still around. We had a little trouble."

Stubblefield looked up. "Oh?" he said softly. "What kind of trouble; lightning?"

Winters grimaced, "Yeah, lightning. Gun-lightning. Circle S stampeded us."

Stubblefield acted as though he'd just been stung. He jerked stiffly up in the chair. "*What!* Why—why—do you mean to say Circle S deliberately stampeded Dallas's reservation herd?"

"Yup," agreed Curly, and turned as someone standing darkly over in the bunkhouse doorway bawled out that supper was ready.

Stubblefield stood up, straightened his vest, stepped closer to Curly and said, "Are you sure it was Circle S?"

"We're certain, Mister Stubblefield. We're certain because we caught the batch of 'em includin' Miss Smith."

"Caught them? What d'you mean—caught them?"

"Just what I said. We caught 'em out on DW range, an' she as well as admitted she done it on purpose too." Curly gazed at the banker for a moment before saying, "That's sort of why I figured Dallas lit out for town this mornin'."

"I see. To go to the law."

"Nope. To get drunk."

Stubblefield looked uncomprehendingly upwards. Curly shrugged. That impatient man over at the bunkhouse called over again, only this time he said if Curly didn't hurry over there wouldn't be anything left. Curly called back indifferently saying he wasn't hungry anyway, then he faced Stubblefield.

" Miss Smith was sort of roiled up when we caught 'em out there. She said some stuff to Dallas that I figured'd make him want to get drunk." At Stubblefield's continuing look of uncomprehending wonderment the rangeboss shrugged. " You've heard the gossip. I'm sure of that. Everyone's heard it, Mister Stubblefield."

" Gossip? What gossip?"

" About Dallas killin' some Union feller at Sabine Pass durin' the war."

Stubblefield didn't speak. He seemed to gradually sag into himself. He closed his little soft mouth and drifted his gaze away from Winters over towards that orange lampglow at the bunkhouse.

" Well," said Curly, stepping off the porch. " You can wait over here if you want, Mister Stubblefield, but I got no idea when Dallas'll be back."

" Wait just a minute," Stubblefield murmured, and turned his head. " Miss Burlette said something about *that*—to Mister Wayne's face?"

" Yes sir. 'Said she thought his way of dealin' with folks he didn't admire was to cut their throats with his Bowie knife, or somethin' like that. I don't recollect the exact words."

" You were there?"

" Well o' course, Mister Stubblefield. Otherwise how'd I know what she said? So was most of the DW crew. We all heard it." Curly put his head slightly to one side and watched Stubblefield a moment, then he said, " An'

I see you've heard that story too. You look like you just swallowed your stogie."

Stubblefield did, in fact, look grey and anguished, but he had nothing more to say so Curly turned and started on over the yard. He paused upon the bunkhouse porch to turn for a rearward look. The banker was slow-pacing his way down to his buggy. Curly waited until he saw Stubblefield untie, climb up in, turned his horse and start on out of the yard. Then he pushed on inside and explained who the caller was.

" Funny thing that he didn't see Dallas in town," he concluded with, and took a cup of coffee which was offered him by one of the other men. " 'Course, I reckon bankers don't hang out much in saloons." The cowboys smiled at that; ordinarily they were stand-offish around bankers—around any town-men who wore neckties and vests and little bowler hats.

" I told him about the stampede," mused Curly nursing his coffee while he thought back. " He acted like someone'd just jabbed him with a hatpin. Liked to have jumped out of his chair."

" Why?" muttered a stocky, swarthy cowboy. " What's it to him, anyway? Them danged bankers think they got to know everything that's goin' on." This same man crossed to the bunkhouse table, sat down and began tugging off his boots. " What'n hell did he want out here anyway?"

Curly finished his java and flung the tin cup over into a bucket of oily dishwater. " He never said an' I never asked."

" Wouldn't have told you anyway," growled the swarthy cowboy. " Them fellers always got to act like everythin' they know is a big old secret. You know what I think? I think bankers are fellers who done got a real

mealy start in life an' figure the only way to hide a
pretty sorry beginnin' is to wear one of them neck-ties
an' a vest, and go aroun' lookin' like they're little tin
gods. One time down in Texas I knew a banker real
well, an' if there ever was a stuffed shirt this feller was
it. Why, one time—"

"Hey," a DW rider who was already in his bunk,
called out protestingly, "why the hell don't you shut up
and go on t'bed. Dallas'll come bouncin' through that
door before sunup tomorrow tickin' off the names of
the fellers who'll have to go north with the reservation
gather, an' if I'm one of 'em I don't want to be all
baggy-eyed for lack of sleep."

Another rider who was similarly already bedded down
heartily agreed with this, so that swarthy man subsided
after a pointed, blistering and unflattering remark about
rangeriders who couldn't miss a few hours' sleep, flung
down his boots and gingerly went over to his own bunk.

Curly Winters sat there at the table sipping coffee,
thinking, and looking caustic. He didn't say anything
but very clearly his thoughts were uncharitable towards
someone.

It wasn't Stubblefield though; he'd already dismissed
the banker from his mind. It was Circle S, Burlette
Smith, Ted Sloan, and the things Burlette had said to
his boss. Curly was not a complicated man. He was
fearless; he was a top-hand and an excellent rangeboss
over both men and animals, but he was neither deep
nor calculating. He awoke each morning in a new world,
rarely carried worries or grudges over from one day to
the next, and was totally loyal to Dallas Wayne.

He didn't *want* to believe that story about Dallas
and the Union secret service messenger. When he'd first
heard it he'd offered to whip the man who'd slyly told

it to him. But Curly Winters was not a fool either; what now was keeping him awake was the same thing which was also keeping Frank Webster awake out at the gather-ground; the thing Curly had mentioned to Frank before leaving the holding-grounds. If Dallas hadn't done that, then how was it that he'd appeared instantly to fully understand what Burlette Smith had meant by her blunt and cruel remark about throat-cutting?

Curly finished his second cup of java, put the cup squarely before him, cupped both hands around it and sat there unmindful of the grunts and groans of his bed-ding-down companions, thinking that now, after all this time, loyalty wasn't enough. He had to find out if there was any truth in that grisly story and its bitter implica-tions or not.

" Hey dammit," someone growled from a wall-bunk. " Curly; put out that doggone lamp and hit the hay, will you !"

Curly stood up, blew down the lamp chimney plung-ing the bunkhouse into darkness, and began to thought-fully shuck his clothing. Out of the darkness a man's quiet Texas voice said : " Curly—you reckon he really *did* do that?"

Winters looked into the blackness thinking he'd re-cognised that voice as belonging to the swarthy cowboy. But he didn't answer. No one answered. There was only the steady rise and fall of men breathing in the room. Not rhythmically breathing as sleeping-men would breathe, but taking in the uneven, deep-down sweeps of breath that men lying in full darkness with their eyes wide open might take, as they pondered something which was coming to more and more trouble their tired minds.

Curly went to the door, opened it and looked out.

This was a habit of his every night, and he afterwards left the door open so they'd have plenty of fresh night-air in the bunkhouse, only this time he didn't peer around then go back to his rope-spring bunk and bed down. This time he stood over there watching the blinding tail-race of a speeding comet until it burnt down to a dull-glowing cinder leaving behind its scratch upon the belly of the Universe, and he too pondered.

Down by the corral a horse blew its nose and another horse, stabled inside the barn, stamped fretfully in his tie-stall. Curly placed these sounds as he turned to cross the still, darkened room, and he muttered a fierce: "Dammit!" not making it clear whether he was growling at the horses or at his unpleasant thoughts.

6

THERE WAS an endless scope for speculation about this matter, and the next day, as well as the days following, people had their say about it, including Dallas Wayne's rangeboss and his other men.

But these men were Texans; some of them, at least the older ones, had cause to remember that war. Some had physical scars, others had mental scars, but the vivid recollections were there, even for the younger men who'd had no part of the combat, for among Texans the policing of their proud, defeated state by Yankee bluebellies still rankled. Tales of atrocities were many and colourful, whether they were true or not.

It was this strictly Texas-viewpoint which kept Dallas' men riding for him. They couldn't condone such a grisly act for such a supposedly immoral reason, but on the other hand he was a Texan and so were they. Therefore, they'd await his word on that story, and until he chose to give it, they'd go right on serving him—and woe to the Virginia City denizen who threw that story up into their faces.

It couldn't be that way for everyone, of course, because Nevada Territory had been, during the war, almost unanimously sympathetic to the Union cause. For those who'd heard the story without any reason to favour an ex-Confederate, there was plenty to hitch their animosity to. For one thing, the have-nots, as always, were delighted to believe the worst of a man who had prospered where they had not. For another thing, human nature being what it was, there were a great many who, unable to form any concrete opinions of their own, were perfectly willing to go along with the majority; there was always comfort and a sense of security in belonging to the herd.

These were not, of course, the sterling characters of the territory, nor even the most affluent nor ambitious, but with gossip it's never the individualists who count, it is instead the overwhelming preponderance of the unimaginative, vicious, unintelligent herd, and Nevada Territory had its share of this kind.

All this struck a man who'd had nearly two decades to ponder it, hard, for whether he was guilty or innocent, whether he was successful and respected now or not, the full weight of spiteful, cruel public opinion was there at every turn and in every bland face, to let him know that people were aware of this monstrous deed attributed to him.

The simplest thing of course would have been for Dallas Wayne to deny it all. To prove, if he could, he wasn't that man they thought he was. But a proud man, especially a *Texan*, had his resistance to justifying himself before saloon hangers-on, liverybarn touts, vicious, small people who would listen and silently jeer. As someone had once said, a man's friends don't need explanations and his enemies won't believe them.

Dallas himself, was brought low by those tart, fierce words Burlette Smith had flung in his face. The story was not a new one to him by any means, and in fact there *had* been such a grisly crime committed. But, sitting in his lonely parlour that night after the angry encounter with Circle S, he chided himself for ever believing that, even though nearly two decades had passed, he'd dared believe the story had died out, been forgotten, and wouldn't be resurrected again.

In wars young men do things older men shun. Sometimes, when the young warriors become older men, they even find shame in their own fevered actions, and that is how Dallas thought that night in the seclusion of his parlour. Whatever he or anyone else had done in those days, now there was only the unhealed and unhealable wounds of the mind to haunt him, to live on, sometimes in secret, sometimes—as now—to spring out of an unexpected place and slash open all the dismal memories over again.

He went out to the gathering ground, saw those solemn, thoughtful expressions and rode back to the home-ranch to get away from them. He went to look at his using-horses and the same bad dream rode his spirit there. He was a little gruff in giving Curly Winters orders for the next day and saw the bewilderment in Curly's eyes over this.

There were a hundred ways for a man to make himself despised by himself, and before Dallas left the ranch for Virginia City he'd come to know most of them.

He wasn't ordinarily a drinking man, not in the sense that he could get drunk and stay drunk for long periods of time. He'd drink like all rangemen drank, sociably to be agreeable, but he'd never been a drunkard. Now though he wanted to get drunk, and perhaps that was ironic because even after he got to town that questionable pleasure eluded him.

He ran into Constable Willett who had a bitter complaint to make of the weather. This normally shouldn't have taken long but with Ben it took long enough because Willett was a man who despised heat, which was sanguinary; no man who professed to hate desert humidity and heat as much as Constable Willett professed to, had any business living in a desert country.

This didn't seem to occur to Willett though. He denounced the heat, the summertime generally, and the thoughtless people who were constantly causing troubles which he had to go iron out—in the hottest part of the day.

Every town had its Ben Willetts just as it also had its bartenders who were acutely aware of their public image as purveyors of liquor to social-drinkers. There was one of these, also, in Virginia City. He in fact was on duty at the Green Door Saloon, and Dallas would have his little brush with this man too, but first he went into a Chinese café run by an ageing celestial with a long, raven-black pigtail, who was something of a celebrity because of an alleged series of secret herb potions which he sold to ranchers, miners, travellers and even townsmen, for the curing of everything under the sun including such rare pestilences as pop-skull hangovers, heat-induced lethargies and incipient pregnancy.

Dallas wasn't particularly hungry but he ducked into the Chinaman's place to get away from Ben Willett, and after he was there, he listlessly ordered a meal. The wrinkled little gnome of a Chinese, very ancient and therefore somewhat experienced, eyed him as he prepared the meal Dallas afterwards didn't touch, and said in nearly flawless English learnt decades earlier in that Chinese melting-pot, San Francisco, that he thought Dallas needed a particular medicine he had in stock which was guaranteed to cure doldrums whatever their cause.

Dallas declined.

The little old Chinese then mixed the potion into Dallas's coffee anyway, and chirped happily to himself over having done good in spite of the patient's demur. Whatever was in that concoction did its work, not quite in the manner the Chinese expected, and certainly not in any way Dallas wanted.

He returned to the roadway, walked on up to the saloon and entered. It was then late afternoon. A thin trickle of early patrons was beginning to show up. Actually though, business would not reach its flourishing, exuberant apex until after nightfall, but when it did, Dallas was still there, gloomy and withdrawn.

Eventually as the hilarity made the walls shake, he took his bottle and retired to a gloomy corner. There he sat with his bitter reflections unmindful of the time.

Men occasionally passed by and nodded, but since he was obviously not in a very sociable frame of mind, while there were plenty of others in the place who were, none of his acquaintances joined him in his gloomy corner, preferring instead the more convivial men elsewhere in the place, either at the tables or up along the bar.

One barman eyed him now and then as the night wore along, but the press of business kept this man from crossing over to Dallas's table, which was just as well.

Constable Willett came in just after midnight, saw Dallas, went on up to the bar, had a drink and watched the gloomy corner over his shoulder through the back-bar mirror. Ben Willett had never before seen big Dallas Wayne steadily drink like this, nor, for that matter, had he ever seen him sitting gloomily alone with quite that expression upon his face.

Willett wondered, his curiosity piqued, but he was not

by nature a meddler even though he'd been a lawman for thirty years, so he occasionally glanced around, but otherwise he didn't go over, or, even when the crowd began to thin out after midnight, offer to give the frankly disapproving barman any sympathy. In old Ben Willett's book if a man wished to drink by himself until he slid down under the table with a total lack of identity, it was fine. One thing Ben wouldn't stand for was trouble. If a drunk caused trouble Ben had a good stout jailhouse available.

But Dallas didn't cause trouble. In fact, he simply sat over there staring into space, occasionally drinking, allowing himself to be infrequently jostled by other, more bubbly patrons of the Green Door Saloon and didn't even look around when this happened.

The barman edged up to Willett, bobbed his head towards Dallas's corner and growled. "That's Wayne, isn't it?" he inquired. "Isn't Wayne just about the biggest cowman and whatnot hereabouts?"

Willett nodded. "That's Wayne," he conceded, "but I don't know about the rest of it. He's got a big ranch northwest of town—called the DW—but I don't know for sure what a big whatnot is."

The barman shot Willett a suspicious dark look. He thought the lawman was talking down to him, was in some veiled way being sceptical of him. "Well I'll tell you this much," he growled. "He don't own that corner table over there. If all he's goin' to buy is one lousy bottle an' nurse it all night, I got a notion to throw him out."

Willett gazed down his nose. He said, "Y'know, friend, if I wasn't any bigger'n you are I'm not right sure I'd try that. I've never seen Dallas Wayne fired up, but I've been around my share of years an' let me tell you, sometimes those big rawboned men like that got a right short fuse. Besides; if he bought a bottle that's more'n most of your other customers have bought, buyin' dime drinks one at a time, so why don't you just tend bar and stay right healthy?"

The barman stalked off leaving Willett to finish leisurely his own ten-cent shot of raw whisky and also to study Dallas over his shoulder.

The noise lessened however, along towards one o'clock and Ben departed. He went out to have a quiet smoke and to make his dutiful rounds of Virginia City. But after that, just out of curiosity, he returned to the Green Door.

There was a younger barman on duty when he came back and this man didn't seem particularly disturbed that Dallas Wayne was still sitting in his corner drinking. He in fact told Constable Willett that as far as he was concerned, since the place remained open twenty-four hours a day, he rather liked the idea of someone sitting out the wee hours with him.

Willett made a sage reply: " I don't figure you're goin' to find Dallas Wayne much comfort tonight. Something's gnawing away at his vitals. I'd advise that you just leave him alone, mind the bar, and when he gets damned good and ready, he'll jump one way or the other; either get up and go out of here and maybe let off a big rebel yell from the centre of the road, and shoot out all the lamplights, or else he'll just go on drinkin' like he's been doin' and cause no one any trouble—providin' they leave him plumb alone."

The younger man said sympathetically, " Suits me, Constable. Suits me right down to the ground. You care for a drink?"

Willett shook a weary head. " No thanks. I'm fixin' to head for home and a good night's rest. I've got a

feelin' when Dallas Wayne comes out of his cocoon sometime tomorrow, I'll be in hot water up to my neck again.
Good night."

"Good night, Constable."

7

THE BARMAN at the Green Door Saloon went away and said to an old grizzled cowman standing in a low slouch down near the bar's farthest ending, "I don't know what's wrong with him," meaning big Dallas Wayne who was up there nursing an amber drink. "Don't think he's gone home since last night."

The old cowman looked up the bar and down into his own whisky glass. "Ain't shaved recent," he observed. "Reckon he's got his troubles."

"What troubles?" snorted the bartender. "What troubles can a man have who's got as much land an' cattle an' other holdings as folks tell me he's got?"

The old cowman kept gazing solemnly down into his glass. "You haven't been around Virginia City long," he stated quietly. "Dallas Wayne's got troubles, don't you never think otherwise." The cowman lifted his glass, downed the liquor and walked on out of the saloon.

There weren't many men in the place, it was too early in the day, but what few strays and idlers were around seemed subdued. They looked over where Dallas was doing his drinking now and then, whispered a little among themselves and shrugged. If a man wanted to get drunk it was fine with them, only they'd never before seen this particular man do that, so they had something to chew on, something to speculate about, and meanwhile Dallas stood over there at the deserted bar drinking and staring at the back-bar mirror, and drinking some more.

There are times, infrequent it's true, when whisky just doesn't do to a man what it's supposed to do. When those extremely rare occasions occur, all liquor does is sharpen a man's perception—and also sharpen his recollections.

Dallas flagged for the disgruntled barman and bobbed his chin at the empty glass. Without a word passing between them the bartender re-filled the glass, started to turn, started to replace the bottle on its shelf, thought better of it, turned back and set the bottle down, hard, and waited. Dallas dredged up some crumpled money. The barman took it and went to his cash-drawer. While his back was turned Dallas downed that drink and reached for the bottle.

The bartender returned and dumped a little heap of silver coins in the sticky puddle. He shot Dallas a look and his thick brows drooped like the black unkempt wings of a bird. He knew drunks and this one could very easily turn maudlin or troublesome. He wanted to throw him out but he didn't because he knew who Dallas Wayne was. Still, he nursed this thought and it made him turn a little sullen; it wasn't good for business to have bleary-eyed drunks in the place regardless of who they were or how much money they were worth. He walked midway down the bar and became busy sluicing out glasses in a bucket of dirty water under the bar.

Some cowboys came in noisily, called for beer, saw Dallas Wayne drinking alone and steadily, took their beers and went over to a poker table with them, suddenly quiet and interested. The barman saw this and it heightened his resentment. He'd only been in Virginia City six months, didn't know all the stories of the people hereabouts, but since he was on a percentage basis one thing he did know was that Dallas Wayne's presence like this wasn't going to improve business any.

He took up a bar-rag and went up to roughly swipe off the spilt liquor and the little puddles where Dallas was stonily leaning. He said, "You had about enough haven't you, Mister Wayne?"

Dallas brought his attention back from some far-off place with a strong effort. He looked into the barman's face, saw the sulkiness there and gradually came to stare at the man. His eyes were dry and dull; they held the barman's glance for a long time before Dallas spoke.

"Get away from me."

The voice was a little hoarse, but it was very soft, almost gentle, and the barman, who clearly fancied himself a capable rough-and-tumble man, leaned forward upon his bar quite deceived by that mildness.

"When a feller gets enough, Mister Wayne, the best thing is to go sleep it off. That's what you ought to do. It ain't good for business, you slobberin' in here."

"I'll tell you once more," Dallas gently said. "Get away from here. Leave me be."

Now it dawned upon the barman that mildness did not necessarily, at least in this case, indicate detachment. Dallas's slouch over the bar had nothing at all to do with his hard stare. He was loose and easy, true, but he was also very near the raw edge of some kind of an explosion, and this the barman had missed entirely right up until now. He straightened back up off the bar turning stiff. His private conviction that he was tough enough took a bad blow from this; it wouldn't let him do the prudent thing though, which would have been to turn on his heel and wisely walk away. At least not right away. So they stood with the bar between them watching one another.

Dallas wasn't drunk; in fact he was a little sick inside and therefore not normal, but he wasn't drunk. He saw the barman's resentment and understood it. He also saw the man's belief in himself begin to crumble. He tossed off another drink and reached once again for the bottle. But he didn't pour because that would have required him to lower his eyes; he simply held the bottle, steadily staring over the bar, waiting.

The complete dissolution of the barman's courage finally occurred. The man swung his head and jerkily walked away. He would never be quite the same man again.

Dallas poured his drink and hooked both elbows over the bar to consider it. The stuff tasted awful but that wasn't what he was drinking it for anyway, the taste. It wasn't getting to him; wasn't doing its job, so he didn't lift the glass again.

He ran a hot palm over the freshly wiped and dampened bartop, found the wood pleasantly smooth and cool, found it oaken and solid, which was comforting, and wondered if there was any counterpart in life to equal that good solidness. Certainly there was none among men. Men came and went, they gave a person their crafty smiles or their oily stares, and they constantly schemed. He, himself, had been like that until there'd no longer been a need for deception. He'd been courtly towards bankers' fat, dumpy wives; had been full of gentle good manners towards merchants and land-barons. He'd even turned the other cheek when every Texas instinct had cried out for him to wade in with both fists swinging.

For what? For a past that wouldn't stay dead and a future that never came? For a bunch of damned dreams of wealth and power which *had* come, almost too easily, and which now meant only that he was a slave to the details of his everyday damned existence?

Once fun had mattered; once he'd laughed and swaggered a little and hadn't had more than two silver dollars to rub together in his pockets. He reached out in his mind to those other, carefree days; to his youth even, which had been full of choking hardship and bleakness, but where the sun had been brighter and where the stars had been sharper. He reached out for the war-years too. Danger and risk and imminent peril had become a habit, an accepted way of life. Faces came rising up out of a twenty-year mist to slyly wink at him, to laugh aloud in total silence, simply to look and look and never show any emotion, then to fade away as eerily as they'd come.

He groped through the kaleidoscope for the scent of burnt cannon powder, for the smell of honest horsesweat and the wonderful odour of campfires where grey-clad Texans hunched around stringy rabbit stew with their old-young lined faces gazing out at him as though through a soiled window, lips drooping, eyes vacantly smiling, faces uncertain and expectant, and with the pallor of near-death upon them.

He put up a hand to squeeze the dryness from his grating eyes, to push aside the dank and unhealthy whisky-sweat upon his unshaven face. A man never went back. Each day of his life he got farther away. His bones changed, his flesh and muscles altered irrevocably until, after near twenty years, he wasn't even the same man. Today's whisky like today's sunsets was altogether different from those earlier searing drinks and those red-gold blazes of light that had once long ago mantled a man's strength and dreams and exultant hopes.

Sabine Pass? That had been another man too, back there. Who, his mind suddenly screamed in terrible silence, who had resurrected that story and brought it here, to far-away Nevada Territory? Who had seen Dallas Wayne in Virginia City after all those years, and remembered that story?

Why would a man not let yesterday stay in its grave?

He pushed back the glass, lowered his head briefly to that cool wood, felt a little better and raised up, turned about and set himself for the long walk over to the door, drew up his wide shoulders, dropped both big arms and started moving.

They were watching him. Everyone was watching him. Not because he was drunk—which he really wasn't —but because, damn them all, *they knew that story!* He was as positive of this as he was of anything. In retrospect for nearly twenty-four hours he'd been thinking back to the period of coolness the fall and winter before, to the quickly averted faces, to the gravely impassive nods, to the little crafty glances, to all the things he'd dispassionately attributed to envy until just twenty-four hours earlier, when the full weight of total understanding had come down upon his brain like the blow of a hammer. *Virginia City knew the story of Sabine Pass!*

He got out into the fresh air and noticed with a slight start that it was no longer full daylight; noticed that dusk was approaching. He should go home, of course, but home to what; an empty house where the same haunting things would be waiting? To Hell with that; he'd stay right here in town. Let them stare and whisper and snicker. Let them . . . Someone had once told him that men could be in hell a long time before they died, and at the time he hadn't quite understood. *Now* he did.

He went down by the bank where there was a wooden bench distrustfully bolted to the wall so no one could carry it off, and sat down to let night build up around him in its shielding, impersonal manner, and oddly enough he thought of Burlette Smith; thought of the savage hatred he'd seen in her wintry stare when she'd seared his soul with that statement about his Bowie knife.

How long had she known? How long had any of them known? It humiliated him to think now that even as he'd been smiling and talking to people, they'd been watching him as though he were a murderer; had been secretly feeling enormously superior despite his wealth and his power. He fisted both his big hands and squeezed his eyes closed until water ran under the lids.

She had judged him long ago. That's why she'd been so contemptuous at the corrals that day Ted Sloan had been hurt. He opened his eyes wide. *That's* what had caused that stupid disagreement over those corralled horses to blow up into a war between them. She'd come out there with her mind already made up about him!

He also thought of Curly Winters, his rangeboss for four years now, a fellow Texan. And Frank Webster too; all his Texan riders. *They had also known!*

A top-buggy spun past through the nightfall. He was conscious of its passing but not of its stopping half a square beyond. He didn't see the short, dumpy man climb out and peer back up at him. Even when Stubblefield came creakily up the plankwalk a little breathless, a little sweaty and uncertain, Dallas didn't look around. Not until the banker murmured his name and said, " I've been out at the ranch trying to find you. I'd like to talk to you, Dallas."

He looked up then, waiting out the length of time it took for full recognition of George Stubblefield to haul him fully back to the present.

" Talk," he said. " What's on your mind?"

" Well. Do you mind if I sit down?"

" I don't mind."

" Uh; thanks."

Stubblefield perched upon the bench twisted a little so that he had a good view of Dallas's greasy, unshaven countenance. It was quite a shock to Stubblefield, who'd never seen big Dallas Wayne in any light except that of a successful man. He looked twenty years older tonight, and dirty. It was quite a shock.

" Well. I saw Burlette as you suggested, about that damage suit she's bringing against you."

" Is that so?" drawled the lanky Texan. " George— let me ask you a question. I want you to give me a straight-out answer. You understand?"

" Yes, of course. What is it, Dallas?"

" George; when did you first hear that I'd killed a man who was carrying secret orders for a truce from Lincoln to Jefferson Davis of the Confederacy?"

Stubblefield choked, pulled out a handkerchief and put it to his fat little lips. His eyes kept getting larger and larger.

Dallas twisted up his mouth in a bitter expression and said, steadily watching the banker, " A straight-out answer, George. Right now!"

" Well," muttered Stubblefield, through his handkerchief. " Well, Dallas . . ."

" Damn you, Stubblefield!"

" All right. A Texas cowboy, an older man, came through Virginia City over a year ago. He told a room full of men up at the Green Door Saloon."

" What was his name?"

" Well. No one thought to ask. He said he'd served with you in Hood's Brigade. Said that he was right there when—that thing happened."

" What else did he say?"

" I wasn't there, Dallas, I only got it second-hand."

" I see. And for a year an' more everyone's known that story."

" Well. Yes, I suppose they have." Stubblefield lowered the handkerchief, leaned a little and said swiftly. " You could deny it. It'd be your word against that drifter's. The people who count would take your word, Dallas."

For a moment Stubblefield got no comment on that, but ultimately Dallas said, " No they wouldn't, George. Neither would you. People believe what they want to believe, especially about men like me who've made their mark quickly." Then Dallas Wayne turned his head and softly said, " Anyway, George—it's true."

Stubblefield's handkerchief went to his mouth again. He sat as though turned to rock. Dallas watched him, saw the horror, the shock, the slow-gathering revulsion in Stubblefield's night-shadowed wide eyes. He nodded at the banker, holding his long-lipped mouth in that bitter, twisted way again.

" It's true, George. If I said it wasn't me who did that, no one would believe it. And why should I? What do I care what you think—what any of you think?"

" Dallas, listen. You've been drinking. I won't say a word of this to anyone as long as I live. Why don't you go on home now, and maybe ride back into town tomorrow or the next day. Then we can discuss this further."

" Why?" said Dallas, drawing up out of his slouch upon the bench. " Why, George? Did you know Burlette threw that in my face? Did you know she stampeded my reservation herd because—not because of what happened to Ted Sloan, George? but because she'd judged me an' condemned me, and now she despises me, and within a few days now all the rest of you will do the same. What is there to discuss? It happened about like you heard. Would you like me to give you the details?"

Stubblefield jumped up, whirled and went trotting swiftly away, back down towards where he'd left his patient-standing horse and his top-buggy. He didn't even look back as he grunted up into the rig, and whipped up his horse.

8

It DIDN'T occur to George Stubblefield until about noon of the following day that he'd quite forgotten to mention to Dallas Wayne why he'd gone to all that trouble to locate him. But this didn't occur to Dallas at all the next day. He recalled saying bitter, wicked things to the banker but that was all he distinctly recalled until he met Curly Winters down at the barn tinkering with some broken harness straps, and Curly told Dallas, without looking directly at him that Stubblefield had been at the ranch seeking him.

"I saw him in town," muttered Dallas, taking forth his stalled horse, cross-tying the beast and going over to lift his saddle with unsteady hands.

Curly turned. He'd screwed up his courage. He watched Dallas pause, then gruntingly heave his saddle over the horse's back. Curly said, "Dallas; something I'd like to know." He said this so quietly, so evenly, that Dallas turned fully around, noting the quiet difference in his rangeboss's voice, and, after turning, seeing the difference as well in Winter's tanned, weathered, square and honest face.

Dallas said, "Sure, Curly. Sure. You talked to Stubblefield last night. You've been thinkin'." Dallas

turned back, re-settled the saddle and groped under the
horse for the fore and aft cinchas. " An' you've been
thinking. Sure; I understand. Only tell me this, Curly—
was it that damned Stubblefield who told you?"

Winters was motionless. His brows dropped down and
drew inward. "Told me what?"

Dallas turned, on the verge of saying something sharp.
His eyes were bloodshot and his hands unsteady. But he
read total ignorance in Curly's face and let off an
audible, rough sigh. " All right. Excuse me," he muttered.
" I thought . . . Well, never mind. What is it you wanted
to ask me?"

" Uh, Dallas; what Miss Smith said to you the other
day out there." Curly's resolution got somehow diluted
and his voice trailed off with uncertainty.

Dallas watched his rangeboss's face. " So it *is* what I
was thinking," he said quietly. "Sabine Pass. Isn't that
it, Curly?"

" Yes, that's it. A feller wonders, sometimes, Dallas."

" Curly do you want to quit? We've worked four years
together. You want to judge me too?"

" I don't judge, Dallas. All I want to know is—is
that story true? I heard it last winter the first time. The
boys've also heard it. But until she said that to you the
other day—well—didn't any of us talk about it."

" And now you're ready to jump one way or the
other, depending on how I answer you."

" You blame me?"

Over in the shoeing shed someone smartly struck an
anvil. This clear and bell-like sound rose up into a
clarion echo.

" No," said Dallas, as that echo diminished. " No,
Curly, I reckon I don't blame you any. A man's got his
beliefs about what's right an' what's wrong an' he's got

to be true to them or he's not much of a man. Well . . ."
Dallas turned, looped his latigo, made it fast, took down
the bridle from his saddlehorn and stepped up to ease
it into the horse's mouth. " It's true, Curly. I don't know
the version you heard, but a man called Dallas Wayne
killed a Union secret service man with dispatches to the
President of the Confederacy from the President of the
Federal Union at Sabine Pass."

" You know what folks say about that, Dallas?"

" What do they say?"

" That it was pure murder; that the Yankee wasn't
armed an' that he was a prisoner of war. An' that his
killer did that so's he could go on profiteerin'; so's the
damned lousy war wouldn't end. An' they say except
for that, and the way those papers was destroyed, maybe
a hundred thousand grey-backs and blue-bellies might
not have died."

Dallas finished bridling the horses before he slowly
turned to face Winters. " I heard that same reasoning
fifteen, eighteen years ago, Curly. That, and a lot worse.
And I'm not goin' to alibi to you now any more'n I
did then."

" Dallas," said Curly Winters in a tight, stricken voice.
" Give a man somethin' to go on. Four years of sweatin'
alongside you buildin' things up gives me the right to
ask that much of you."

" Listen Curly, I've got to ride out today. Let me
think about this."

Dallas turned, toed in and started to rise up across
his saddle. A bulky oilskin packet fell from his pocket.
He didn't see this until Curly stepped over, picked the
thing up and held it out. Dallas took it, looked at his
rangeboss and nodded. " Thanks. Didn't know I dropped
it . . . Curly?"

" Yeah?"

" Ride out an' tell Frank to send any four of the men you an' he decide upon, to take the reservation beef northward."

" Sure, Dallas."

" And Curly . . ."

" Never mind. Take as much time as you want," Winters said, turned and walked on out back towards the corrals.

Dallas eased down across leather, hooked his booted feet into the stirrups and slowly turned his horse. His throat felt dry, but it was a good feeling. He knew how the indecision was tormenting Curly Winters, and yet it warmed him all the way through that the rangeboss was putting up his private battle to believe in Dallas Wayne.

He left the yard riding due westward and automatically his thoughts ran to the things which had for some years now claimed all his attention. That herd he'd sent to rails-end for example. He wondered if there'd been any mishaps. If the men he'd hired had loaded the cattle without difficulty. He was sure they had. They were the same men he'd used for that same purpose last year and the year before.

And the reservation beef. It didn't much matter who among his riders Curly picked to send with that herd either, because all his riders had made that trip before too. There was of course the two-day delay, occasioned by having to sweat-out another gather after Circle S had caused that stampede, but he was easy in his mind about the delivery date being met. About the only thing he knew of which could cause havoc again would be a lightning storm, and it was too early in the season for that.

Finally, he thought of George Stubblefield, the business he did with the bank, some little odds and ends such as the mortgage he had on the Green Door Saloon which was a month past due now, and that business about the logger Brannan, and these things naturally led him around to thinking of his current trouble with Burlette Smith.

He didn't really know her, had never had occasion to know any of the Smiths very well. Their ranges bordered for several miles but there'd never before been any unpleasantness about that. Not while old Burl or his brothers were alive. As for Sloan—Dallas shrugged thick shoulders as he rode along—Sloan was nothing; a taciturn quarter-blood of some kind with the limited, erratic intelligence of white and red low-castes. The west had its share of men like Sloan. Physically brave, morally straight, good men with livestock but otherwise not much smarter than the horses they rode or the cattle they herded. And vindictive.

He pushed Sloan back and thought of Burlette. She was very attractive. He'd seen her before but this fact hadn't registered those other times. Attractive and tough and willing to fight a man on the man's own ground. Of course that wasn't very smart; women just didn't possess the steel or sinew to fight as men fought. As for this ridiculous law-suit . . . He spotted another rider far out dusting it across his onward route and put everything else out of his mind to watch the stranger.

It wasn't one of his DW men and he didn't think it was a Circle S man although he was now very close to the DW—Circle S boundary. For one thing, that distant man wore a small-brimmed black hat and a dark coat, things rangemen didn't wear except perhaps when they headed for town of a Sunday morning. Another thing, that man didn't sit his horse with the total ease of a cowboy.

The rider cut around northwestward leaving a lazy little trail of grey dust behind him. He was heading in the correct direction to strike Circle S yard perhaps a half hour ahead of Dallas. It finally occurred to Dallas who that stranger might be, and he made a face over that: Burlette's attorney.

He could perhaps have overtaken the other man if he'd chosen to punish his horse to that extent, but it was hot, the race would have been hard, and in the end he thought the lawyer would still be there when he rode in anyway.

He wanted a look at this man; wanted to find out whether or not George Stubblefield had given the stranger Dallas Wayne's proposition—or ultimatum, whichever he chose to consider it.

The rider swept ahead out of sight, his dust began to settle, the land became as empty as before except for an occasional glimpse of DW cattle, and later on, Circle S cattle, so he reverted to those reveries which had been interrupted by the stranger's rushing across his onward path.

He'd ridden perhaps a mile, perhaps slightly more than that when he came upon the tracks another man had made. These held his interest briefly as he steered his mount along parallel to them, but there was nothing very outstanding about fresh, shod-horse marks upon the summer-hard earth, so he thought about Burlette again.

Did all women pre-judge men? That was it, of course. That's what had her back up the day they'd first tangled over those loose horses her men had corralled. She'd already made up her mind about him before they ever came together over there. Except for that, and her antagonism, there probably wouldn't have been any trouble. The same applied to this silly lawsuit. She was striking back at him, was lashing out at the image of him she'd come to detest wholeheartedly, without making any actual effort to see him, to talk to him, to try and actually ascertain just what kind of man he was.

That was why he was riding to Circle S today. Not because George Stubblefield had suggested it. That was also why he'd brought along that oilskin packet of papers, too. No man, regardless of his wealth or his position, cherished having people pre-judge him. But, where most powerful men wouldn't bother trying to correct what would appear to them to be the manifiestation of a little mind, Dallas Wayne would take that time out of a busy schedule. He'd decided to do this sometime the night before and his reasoning was elemental. Spite had turned to something more physical between DW and Circle S. That stampede hadn't hurt him, but what would follow it could hurt a lot of people because his Texans were angrily resentful now too. It would be only a matter of time before Curly or Frank or some of his other hair-triggered men bumped into Sloan or some of her other hands in Virginia City.

So he was riding now to head off that kind of serious trouble. It wasn't anything he wanted to do and he had his personal reasons for not wanting this, but no wise man ever let smouldering grass roar up into a raging brush fire, either. He'd made the bitter decision the night before.

Where those fresh shod-horse tracks abruptly veered northward he kept going due westward. It was his wish to ride into the Circle S yard from down-country. To come in from behind the big old main house. This way, he was sure he'd avoid meeting her riders until after he'd seen her.

It was good thinking except for one thing. Although he wished to avoid violence with Sloan and the other resentful Circle S men, they didn't wish to avoid violence with him. He was a mile away when the faint scent of acrid dust rode the still air bringing up his awareness. But before he could discern from which direction this evidence of riders was coming, a gunshot smashed the stillness with its flat, vicious report. Dallas's horse flinched. Less than a second later another gunshot sounded. This time the horse under him jerked up its legs and fell without a sound or a quiver, shot through the head.

He lit on his feet, sprang clear, dropped down to tug at his booted carbine, found the gun hopelessly weighted down under his dead horse, and dropped flat when two more shots broke little limbs off a sage bush five feet to his left.

The horse offered all the protection he had. It wasn't much but it was adequate as long as those unknown assassins out there didn't slip around behind him where he was totally exposed.

He drew his .45, lay it across the dead animal's upper side, and waited. There were several dozen flourishing sage bushes hereabouts, any or all of them were amply capable of hiding one man or five men. He thought, as he lay there waiting and probing, that no more than two men were out there. He also had time to figure out how this ambush had occurred. That rider he'd seen earlier had passed the word at Circle S of a rider approaching from the east. Those bushwhackers out there waiting for another shot at him, had gotten astride, had ridden out here to identify him, and had probably then and there made up their minds what to do. They could be any two of Circle S's men; perhaps a couple of the men he and his own riders had humiliated that day when they'd caught Burlette. They could also be Ted Sloan and one other. It wasn't really important just yet *who* they were; what *was* important was their present intentions towards him. Sloan, he believed, was capable of killing him over that broken wrist. Indians thought like that.

He decided to risk a shot, paused to select which brush clump appeared the most likely to be concealing a watcher, cocked his .45 and squeezed the trigger. He'd fired low and into the leafy centre of the bush. Little dry leaves fell, the bush quivered, but no one cried out, jumped clear or fired back.

He withdrew the gun, kept his head down until he'd punched out that spent casing and plugged in a fresh load from his shell-belt, then set his back to the dead horse and made a long, careful study of the round-about countryside. He thought the reason he hadn't drawn an answering gunshot was because his ambushers were no longer out there ahead of him, which meant they were sneaking around to flank him, or else had departed, satisfied to have set him afoot.

There wasn't a sound anywhere. It was, in fact, un-naturally quiet. Sweat ran down into his eyes. He shook it off. The sun was fiercely hot and bitterly yellow.

9

He half believed that he'd been set afoot as a warning to come no closer to Circle S, and yet, because he'd once been a trained soldier, he kept his close attention upon the places of vantage roundabout. He wasn't willing to believe Sloan would let him walk away so easily; even if Sloan didn't mean to kill him, Sloan would surely wish to mark him some way.

The alternative to lying there feeling falsely secure behind that dead horse, was to crawl over into the brush also, which he did, getting safely clear of the sprawled animal. Four years of war had taught Dallas Wayne and many tough Texans like him, that the secret of combat was never to remain upon the defensive for the elemental reason that a man defending himself was never capable of being offensive to his enemies and all victories were won by offence not defence.

He worked his way through the spiny, flourishing sage until he was well westerly of where he'd been brought down. Then he ducked and darted, hesitated here and there, ran and crawled, northward. He was certain, if those men were still around, they'd come from the northward; that their saddle animals would still be northward.

It was a good guess.

He never did encounter the ambushers again, at least not down where he'd been put afoot or westerly of that spot, but he did eventually locate two saddled horses a mile back tied to a red-barked tall manzanita bush, and he settled down up there and smiled to himself as he began his long vigil. Sooner or later those hunters would return to ths spot. He would be waiting.

The sun burnt down, sweat ran in rivulets under his shirt, thirst annoyed him, time ran on, little watery shadows crept out around the sage clumps, and his would-be assassins did not appear.

It was a long, grim wait. Those ambushers were dogged men. He could imagine them combing the underbrush for him. He also speculated on what they'd meant to do if they'd found him back there in the vicinity of his dead horse. Finally, he made up his mind that *he* wasn't going to walk all the way back to his headquarters ranch. Not as long as there were two horses at hand.

It was more than an hour later before he heard those men coming back. They weren't being careful. He heard them talking grumpily back and forth, heard them boldly striding through the underbrush. One of them said in a voice Dallas did not recognise, that maybe Wayne had gotten away, but by gawd he had one hell of a long walk back to his own ranch, so, even though they hadn't gotten to work him over, at least they'd made him suffer.

The second voice *was* recognisable. It belonged to Ted Sloan, Circle S's foreman, and it was flintily disagreeable. " I still want a crack at him, whether he managed to slip away or not."

" But hell," protested the other bushwhacker, " we

ain't got the time, Ted. We got to get back. He could be anywhere out here hidin' in the brush. It'd take until after dark to find him on foot. Can't even track a man when the ground's this blasted hard."

Sloan said something in a low growl which Dallas didn't understand, then he and his burly, unshaven companion emerged through the brush into the half-acre clearing around that manzanita bush where the horses were tied, and Dallas unwound up off the ground, pushed forward his cocked .45 and said quietly, " Thought I'd save you boys the bother of huntin' for me."

Sloan spun around with his right hand moving. His thick-set companion did the same, but this man, looking squarely into that gun-barrel, froze. Sloan's hand hung rigid, the fingers convulsively closed about his holstered sixgun.

" Go ahead," Dallas said agreeably. " Draw it if you think you can beat a royal flush."

Sloan didn't complete his draw. He too stood motionless, his muddy dark eyes blazing with astonishment and recognition.

Dallas studied the pair of them. He was very calm and very deadly at this moment. He would shoot to kill if anything happened. It took no great powers of divination for his captives to understand this. They returned his stare without so much as seeming to breathe.

" You," Dallas said to the thick-set man. " Drop your gun-left handed."

The Circle S man obeyed. He was, as Dallas had anticipated, one of the riders who had been with Burlette Smith that day Sloan had stampeded DW's reservation herd. He was a small-eyed, battered individual with a low, broad forehead, sunk-set eyes and a cruel mouth.

Dallas nodded at Sloan. "Now you—drop it left-handed."

Sloan was slow to obey. He still wore a soiled bandage upon his right wrist. When he dropped his gun he started to say something. Dallas snarled, silencing him. "You said you still wanted a crack at me, Sloan. Well; you're going to get it right now." Dallas lowered his gun, eased off the cocked hammer and jerked his head at the thick-set man. "Take off your shell-belt, mister, and tie Sloan's hands behind his back with it. Then use his belt to lash both his ankles."

"Hey, what the hell," protested the cowboy. "What you figurin' to do, Wayne?"

"Do? You heard him, he wants another chance at me. But first you and I are going to settle our little difference and I don't want Sloan loose to jump in. Now tie him!"

As the thick-set, burly man unbuckled his belt he turned to run a speculative, crafty look up and down big Dallas Wayne. He made a bleak little confident smile and said, "You figure on doin' this with fists, Mister Wayne?"

"I do. That all right with you, cowboy?"

"That's fine by me, Mister Wayne. Just fine. Here Ted, put your hands in back of you." The cowboy broadly smiled. He dropped one eyelid at Sloan and raised it. His smile was sly and knowing and fully confident. He clearly was an old hand at brawling and was very pleased at the present turn of events.

Sloan too, seemed to lose a lot of his stiffness. He didn't smile at all but when he spoke to Dallas his voice registered confidence. "You've been askin' for this a long time, big man," he sarcastically exclaimed. "And when Jake's finished it's my turn. Think you can walk

over folks, sick your back-shootin' riders on 'em, make
trouble for Miss—"

" Who, Sloan. Who's a back-shooter? You and your
friend here bushwhacked me today. Who are *you* calling
back-shooters?"

" That day at our corrals. One of your riders clouted
me from behind."

Dallas shook his head at Sloan, bracing into the cold
fury of the 'breed's glare. " I don't know how that
happened, but I'll tell you one thing: *I* don't have any
back-shooters working for me, and maybe when I'm
through here, Miss Smith won't have any working for
her."

The burly rider called Jake knelt with his back to
Dallas. He had Sloan's shell-belt with which he made
two wraps around the foreman's ankles. As he did this
he said over his shoulder, " Mister Wayne, you better
be savin' your breath." He said this with a sly look upon
his flat, coarse face, and as he rose up facing Sloan he
winked again. Then he whipped around and sprang.

Dallas wasn't prepared.

" Bust him," cried Ted Sloan. " Break his back, Jake."

Jake was several inches shorter than Dallas but in
weight he had a slight edge. He was compactly put
together, heavily boned and heavily muscled. He'd made
that rapid rush for just one purpose and the minute
Dallas felt those massive arms closing around his middle
he understood why. But Jake didn't pin both Dallas's
arms, which was a mistake. He did, however, get his
hands clasped behind Dallas's back above the kidneys,
and he reared back lifting Dallas a foot off the ground.
The cords in Jake's neck bunched and stood out. His
breath whistled past parted lips as he constricted both
those powerful arms. This bear-hug was one of the

oldest and most successful holds, but it required two things; a lot of physical power, which Jake had, and it also required that the man it was being applied to, had both his arms pinned to his sides, which wasn't the case here.

Dallas swept back a big breath just before those great-corded arms cut off his wind. He could stand the pressure for perhaps ten or twenty seconds, which was all he needed.

He raised his right arm, aimed with a thick thumb, and jabbed. Jake bawled in pain and forced his head down. His left eyeball had been hurt. He clung to Dallas increasing his squeezing pressure. Dallas got his palm under Jake's jaw and set himself to raise the heavier man's head. It was a fierce struggle. Jake's neck was thick, his shoulders rose up to resist also, and Dallas had to lever upwards with his palm slipping with the other man's oily sweat. Ted Sloan cried out breathlessly as Jake's head began to come up.

"Keep down, Jake! Get clear of his palm, keep down!"

Jake tried. He knew what was coming and he even relaxed his bear hug a little in order to resist more fully that lifting pressure. A man's neck, as long as it's bent forward has power, but once it's bent upwards enough to rest squarely upon its supporting backbone, is almost without any power at all.

Jake's head rose steadily. The cords in Dallas's neck stood out, his mouth was wide open and the fierce pressure in his chest was beginning to rise up into his head, was beginning to produce little vivid lights before his eyes. He set himself for the final massive effort and panted. Jake's head came all the way up, and if Jake had had a lick of sense he'd have let Dallas go and would have sprung clear, but he didn't. He glared almost eyeball to eyeball with Dallas Wayne. His head tilted at last and there was no longer any force to his straining.

That was when Dallas jerked his palm clear and jabbed savagely at Jake's right eye with his thumb. That was also when Jake, blinded and in excruciating agony, let go, staggered back and raised both hands to his injured eyes.

Dallas dropped to one knee, put a hand forward to steady the spinning ground, and sucked in great amounts of air. Ted was yelling for Jake to jump in, to rush Wayne, to put the boots to him, and without any question if Jake had been able to do that, the battle would have ended then and there. But Jake's lacerated eyeballs were dripping water, he couldn't see clearly, and so he made no attempt to do as Sloan was profanely ordering him to do.

Dallas stayed down on one knee even after those little multi-coloured lights faded before his eyes. He began breathing normally again, and he turned from watching Jake to studying Ted Sloan. The rangeboss was hopping towards Jake, pleading and cursing. Dallas stood up, wiped both hands and started forward. Sloan saw him coming and ceased his frantic hopping, ceased also his wild cursing.

Dallas came across, lifted an arm and back-handed Ted Sloan off balance. He fell backwards and gasped; he'd fallen squarely upon his bandaged right wrist. He groaned, rolled off and sat up with his jaw muscles locked hard against an obvious urge to cry out from pain. His black eyes were fixed upon Dallas Wayne with an unrelenting urge to kill moving in their depths.

But Dallas set his back to Sloan, caught Jake by one

shoulder, half spun him around and swung from the
belt. Jake sagged clear and the blow missed, but that
had been an instinctive thing Jake had done. He still
kept his face covered. He was defenceless. Dallas stepped
in, buried a blasting fist into Jake's middle, struck him
behind the ear as Jake cried out and doubled over, pawed
him off and struck him alongside the jaw even as Jake's
hands were falling, as he was already going down.

It was all over.

Dallas drew back a big breath, gazed upon the badly
beaten Circle S man, bent, scooped up Jake's hat and
dropped it over the unconscious man's injured eyes. He
then straightened around to watch Ted Sloan try to inch
along where two sixguns were wickedly glistening under
the fierce yellow sun.

" Hold still," he ordered, neither raising his voice nor
moving to intercept Sloan. " You want to try your luck
with a gun, hold still until I set you loose, then we'll
both start from scratch."

Sloan twisted as Dallas came over to him, bent and
freed Sloan's ankles. He sat perfectly motionless too
when Dallas freed his wrists, caught Sloan by the
shoulder and yanked him upright, stepped back and
pointed to the guns upon the ground.

" Take your pick, Sloan. Because your right hand's
hurt I'll square it up with you. I won't draw until you've
got the gun in your left hand."

Sloan looked down where those flung-aside weapons
lay. The will to kill was tight across his swarthy face, it
was a bright light in his obsidian eyes. But he didn't
move.

" Go ahead," urged Dallas. " This is the way you
wanted it. Go ahead, pick it up."

The 'breed let his breath out in a tight, low whistle.

"I can't," he said. "Not with my left hand. I never could aim or shoot left-handed. Damn you, Wayne."

Dallas hooked both thumbs in his shell-belt and gazed steadily upon the rangeboss. "Then how?" he asked. "You want a chance and I'm willin' to see you get one. But how?"

Sloan raised his savage glare and swore at Dallas. He had nothing to suggest as an alternative. He was crippled and they both knew it. He was brick-red with wrath, but there was nothing he could do about that either, so he simply, frustratedly, cursed.

Dallas shook his head. "That's not hurting me and it's not helping you. How bad's that wrist?"

"It cracked again when I fell backwards on it. But I'll get you, Wayne. I give you my word I'll kill you."

Dallas shrugged, looked over where Jake was softly whimpering, said, "Next time bring at least five Circle S men with you, Sloan. It'd take that many. Now put your pardner on his horse and head back with him." Dallas looked around. "You walk. I'll borrow your horse to get home on. If you want him after that—if you've gots the guts to come get him—I'll have him corralled at DW. And Sloan, one more thing: you tell Miss Burlette I was on my way to talk to her; to show her something. It might be to her advantage to see me, but you better also tell her that from today on if my men catch any Circle S riders on DW range—they'll have orders to shoot first and talk afterwards. Now get the hell out of my sight!"

10

THE HORSE Dallas 'borrowed' from Ted Sloan was a young animal still in the hackamore. He walked out with a good willingness but he had that coltish propensity to shy at shadows and little birds flitting through the underbrush which made it necessary for Dallas to ride him every inch of the way back to his home place instead of relaxing as he'd have done on an older animal, such as the one which had been shot out from under him.

He had those two sixguns he'd taken from Sloan and Jake pushed into his waistband. They didn't make for comfortable riding but he'd had no intention of leaving them behind.

The last view he'd had of the Circle S men was before the sun had noticeably begun to fall off centre. Sloan had been walking ahead of the horse Dallas had left behind, leading that animal while Jake had sat up there holding a wet and filthy handkerchief across his bruised eyes.

It had been a rewarding sight. He'd thought at the time it would also be a shocking sight when those two battered cowboys got back to Circle S with their humiliating story of being beaten by one man after first having had him in their sights.

By the time Dallas got back to the ranch there were long shadows walking down the land. He put up his

Circle S horse and strolled out of the barn just as Curly
Winters and Frank Webster came jogging in from the
north. Those two had been talking, but at sight of Dallas
they stopped this, slowed to a steady onward walk, and
stared. Finally, when they were close enough to halt and
swing down, Curly said, "What in the hell happened
to you?"

Dallas looked down at himself. His clothing was dirty.
It also was torn. "Had a fight," he said, looking
up. "Got bushwhacked over on Circle S range by a rider
named Jake—and Ted Sloan."

"Bushwhacked!" gasped tough and taciturn Frank
Webster. "Why them lousy no account sons of—"

"It worked out all right," broke in Dallis, and jerked
a thumb over his shoulder towards the barn's shady in-
terior. "I rode Sloan's horse back. They killed the horse
I was riding."

Frank swore with feeling and got violent in the face.
He was a hot-tempered man at best, but this unprovoked
ambushing of Dallas Wayne was more than he could
stomach. "Let's round up the boys an' go do a little
house-cleanin'," he exclaimed. "I never did cotton to
that danged 'breed foreman Circle S's got. As for some
of them other riff-raff *she* hires, I'd as leave bust 'em
open like rotten melons as—"

"We're not going anywhere," growled Dallas, scowling darkly at Webster. "But from today on I want every
man on my payroll to sprout eyes in the back of his head.
If any strangers appear on our range—shoot. You two
pass that word around." Dallas relaxed, shot a look
northward, and in an altogether different tone of voice,
said, "Curly; who went with the reservation herd?"

"Slim as straw-boss; Bob, Trevor, Houston, an—"

"Why not Frank?"

Curly looked down then up again. He clearly didn't wish to discuss this, but, under Dallas's waiting stare, he now had to, so he said, " Well; 'peared to me, Dallas, like there wasn't likely to be no trouble on that drive."

" And you figured there just might be some trouble around here."

" Well . . ."

" Hey," spoke up Frank Webster, half turned and squinting southeastward. " Buggy comin'."

Curly looked relieved about this. Whoever was driving that rig had just more than likely saved him from having to say something he didn't particularly want to say.

Dallas stood a long time watching that oncoming outfit before he swore mildly under his breath and said flatly, " Banker Stubblefield. I reckon he just remembered what it was he came out here last night to see me about." He turned on his heel and started across towards the main house. " Got to clean up. You boys take his horse for him."

Frank and Curly nodded. They stepped inside the barn with their own animals, began to off-saddle, and had this chore completed long before George Stubblefield came wheeling up outside in the gathering soft gloom of early evening, gave them both a solemn " Good evening ", and grunted down out of his buggy.

Curly took the horse, loosened its check-rein, looped the lines and left the animal to be led off by Frank. As he turned as though to walk off, George Stubblefield said, " Just a moment, friend. Is Dallas at home this time?"

Curly jerked a thumb towards the main house without speaking.

Stubblefield walked up to him, smiled and looked up

into the taller, leaner and younger man's face. "Did you tell him I was out here last night, son?" he enquired.

"I did. But he said he saw you in Virginia City last night anyway, Mister Stubblefield."

"Well, yes. But we didn't get to talk."

Curly shrugged and jerked his thumb towards the house again. "You can talk all you like now, Mister Stubblefield. He just come in about a half hour back and went on over to clean up." Curly turned and this time kept on walking towards the bunkhouse. Behind, where he'd left the banker, Stubblefield hitched at his trousers, swept back his coat and headed straight across the yard towards the house. There was a lamp burning over there in some back room. It didn't cast much of a glow because it wasn't dark enough yet for that, but it clearly indicated that someone was inside, so Stubblefield stepped up onto the porch, crossed to the door and sharply rapped. Down at the barn Frank Webster, watching all this, leaned upon the doorless opening and wryly shook his head. Bankers! Of all the useless leeches under the sun . . . Frank pushed upright and started ambling on over to the bunkhouse where another light was guttering to life and where men's voices began to rise through the shadows of another finished long day.

Stubblefield had to knock again before Dallas came out to open the door. He'd washed, combed his hair and was wearing a fresh shirt. Stubblefield, with no inkling there'd been any additional trouble between Circle S and DW, smiled.

"Have something to tell you," he said, through that uncertain small smile.

Dallas stepped out onto the veranda, motioned Stubblefield to a chair and took one himself. As the pair of them sat down the banker's smile dwindled, he studied Dallas's shadowed features and cleared his throat. Clearly, whatever conversation was in prospect here, he was going to have to undertake.

" I talked to Miss Smith," he said, and watched Dallas's face come around. " She brought her attorney to the bank."

Dallas said : " When?"

" Yesterday."

Dallas looked away again, looked out across his ranch yard where gentle starshine was beginning to take up where dying daylight had atrophied. He relaxed in his chair and pushed both long legs out.

" I took her attorney aside and told him what you'd said."

" And he didn't like it," Dallas suggested in a soft murmur.

" No, he didn't. Not at first. Not until I told him that you weren't at all pleased with his wish to bring the damage suit to court, and suggested that he talk over with you the several alternatives."

" Meaning bribes."

Stubblefield's fat shoulders rose and fell. " I didn't use that word. In fact I don't like that word. What I inferred was exactly what you inferred to me; that if he pushed for a court hearing you were likely to take an extremely dim view of his aggressiveness."

" Is he coming to see me?"

" Yes. He said he'd drive out today or tomorrow."

Dallas stroked his jaw thinking back to seeing that stranger riding to Circle S earlier this same day. It wasn't ethical for him to offer to bribe an attorney but it wasn't ethical, either, for the lawyer to evidence interest in such a bribe. The fact that he'd ridden to Circle S before Sloan and Jake had pulled their bonehead play, just might mean anything—that the lawyer had told Burlette of his offer, or that the lawyer didn't tell her.

" I'll be around all day tomorrow waitin' for him," Dallas said, and leaned forward as though to arise.

" I'd like to make a suggestion," said Stubblefield swiftly. " I'd like to suggest that you ride over and see her."

Dallas turned. " I tried that today, George, and a couple of her men shot the horse from under me and also tried to shoot me."

Stubblefield's jaw dropped. His eyes popped wide open. " No," he whispered.

Dallas smiled. " Well; if it was my imagination it sure was realistic." He stood up. " I tried, George, so now *you* try."

" What d'you mean?"

" Go see her; tell her I tried seeing her and didn't quite make it. Tell her I'll be home tomorrow if she wants to ride over and talk." Dallas's voice turned corn-husk dry. " You might also tell her that if it's a war she wants I can promise her a mighty good one. I'm a little prickly about bein' shot at. I think most folks are."

Dallas was moving towards the front door when Stubblefield sprang up. The very thing he'd feared right from the start was now here—a range-war between Circle S and DW. It wasn't altogether the certain violence which made him fearful, it was that other thing; that certainty of who would win and what the terms of capitulation would be for Circle S—the Smith stock in his bank.

" Wait," he said hastily. " Dallas; suppose you ride over there with me. I think if the pair of us—"

" George, when a man gets shot at he's a fool to ride

right back the very next day to where it happened. You aren't allowed very many chances in this life. Using them up like that can damned well get you killed. No thanks. Besides, *I* tried to make peace. Now it's her turn."

Dallas entered the house, softly closed the door and left the banker standing out there upon the porch. It wasn't so much an act of rudeness as it was an act of disapproval of everything Stubblefield had thus far failed to accomplish, and Stubblefield took it that way, too, as he slowly turned and slowly shuffled down across the yard towards the barn.

He began to resent Dallas's attitude towards him even before he led his buggy-horse out of the barn, set the lines and clambered up inside the rig. He was definitely still in the middle, still cast in the unbecoming role of mediator, peace-maker, trouble-shooter. He pursed his lips and glowered over towards the house. His resentment became something stronger than that; it became violent antagonism towards this man who had so handily usurped his power of using other people, and was using him.

Actually, George Stubblefield was no intellectual match for Dallas Wayne. He probably unconsciously knew this, but he'd never admit it to himself, so he whipped up the horse and went rattling out of the yard blaming Dallas Wayne for using him, and for nothing further than that.

On the bunkhouse porch one tobacco-wreathed shadow leaning upon the wall said to another tobacco-wreathed shadow sitting upon a tilted back chair, " Dallas's went and stuck a burr under that feller's blanket. He was mad."

The other shadow opined that Stubblefield, mad or

cheerful, was nothing to worry about. But his friend slouching along the wall said, " I knew a banker once, down in Texas, and let me tell you, Curly, they got ways. Believe me, pardner—they got ways."

Curly snorted quietly, his voice derisive. " What can a feller like that do to a man like Dallas is fixed? Hell; it's the other way around, Frank. If Dallas took a notion he could crack that bank wide open."

Webster smoked for a while, killed his cigarette underfoot and stepped away from the wall. " Reckon I'll go look in on the horses," he casually said, moving towards the steps leading off the porch. " An' don't you never underestimate bankers, boy. Any time men handle the wealth of other folks, they got a hand in things plumb up to the elbow. Don't misunderstand me, though. I got no use for 'em. In fact I got no use for doctors or lawyers either. Got no use for anyone who thrives off the misery of other folk. But for bankers I reckon I got the least use of all. They get their hooks into a man's purse an' from there on they figure they control every breath a man takes."

Curly's lips slowly parted in a wide grin. " How d'you know about that, Frank; you're like me—you never had enough in your cussed purse to interest a banker—only a bartender."

Frank grinned back, shook his head and went shuffling off towards the barn and corrals. Curly finished his smoke, stomped it out and got up out of his chair. It was a serene, beautiful night. He stood there breathing in deeply of that fragrant air. Overhead a million stars steadily shone. A man, he thought, came from the same place as those stars; what was his purpose, what was his reason?

A gunshot exploded down in the barn. It sounded

muffled but there was no mistaking what it was. Curly spun half around. Behind him the bunkhouse door opened and several heads poked out.

" Hey, Curly, was that a gunshot or was we just imaginin' things?"

Curly didn't answer. An awful premonition squeezed around his heart like a constricting steel band. He jumped off the porch and started running. Those cowboys in the doorway moved out onto the porch. One of them swore in a puzzled, nettled way, and also started running towards the barn. The last man out of the bunkhouse started ahead, fetched up short, ducked back inside and emerged again with his carbine. Then he too trotted over towards the barn.

At the main house Dallas had also heard that throaty, muffled explosion. He blew out his parlour lamp, stepped outside onto the porch, saw his riders rushing towards the barn, and with the same premonition Curly'd had, he stepped down into the dust and hiked swiftly onward through that pleasant, pewter starshine.

Somewhere westerly several horses jumped out over rock-like summer-hard ground and sped away. Dallas heard them but his men, already in the barn and throwing harsh words back and forth as Curly Winters held a match high, did not hear them.

One of the riders got a lantern, lit it and hung it upon a saddle-peg. Under this naked light the talk abruptly ceased and the restless movement came to an end.

Dallas appeared in the doorless big, square opening. Only one or two of his DW riders looked up. Curly was one of them. At Curly's feet lay a slumped body, half upon its side, half twisted over onto its back.

" Frank," stated Curly, as Dallas moved towards him.

" He's dead, Dallas. Shot through the heart. He never knew what hit him."

Dallas paused long enough to recognise Webster's orange-lighted features, then dropped to one knee. He didn't feel for a pulse or bend close to watch for the twitching of eyelids. He didn't have to; that sticky, scarlet spot directly in the centre of Frank's shirt said all that had to be said.

Dallas looked up and around. His riders, some only partially dressed, looked back blankly. Curly said, " We was havin' a smoke on the porch when the banker drove out. Frank said he'd have a look at the horses, then turn in. He come down into the barn. I was fixin' to turn in myself when I heard the shot."

" Someone was waitin' in the barn," a rider muttered.

Dallas stood up, stepped over Webster's body and went slowly along the tie-stalls. He stopped and said, " Curly, what horse was tied in here?"

" That one you brought back today. That Circle S horse. Why; ain't he there now?"

Dallas shook his head.

II

FRANK WEBSTER had been a popular man. He'd been straw-boss when Curly wasn't around. He'd been rough at times and he'd also showed a fierce temper when aroused, but he was square and generous and understanding; the riders liked him. His killing didn't sit at all well with them. They took him back to the bunkhouse, put him on his bunk and they forgot all about sleep as they got dressed, stoked up the stove-fire and made a fresh big pot of coffee.

Dallas went back with them. He didn't say what he was thinking but he didn't have to. The others had already pieced together what they were satisfied had happened.

Frank had innocently walked into the barn as someone was untying that Circle S horse to lead it away. Frank may have seen that man, probably had recognised him although it was gloomy inside the barn at night. But one thing was certain; whoever that man was, he'd recognised Frank, and had shot him.

"He shouldn't have took the damned horse," a rider said from over by the stove. "Except for doin' that wouldn't none of us be pretty near sure who shot Frank."

Another man muttered that the killer wasn't thinking

straight; that he'd been caught flat-footed and reacted on the spur of the moment; saw someone facing him and went for his gun. There was a little quiet discussion about this, pro and con, for a while.

Dallas listened, said nothing, and accepted a tin mug of coffee Curly Winters brought over and set before him at the table. Curly sat down across from Dallas with his own cup and didn't say anything right away, but ultimately he did, and the other men around the big bunkhouse listened because clearly, Curly'd arrived at some decisive opinions.

" Sloan," said Curly Winters. " I got no idea exactly why, but for some reason he didn't want that Circle S horse over here at DW."

Dallas gazed across the table. This had also been his conclusion, but he didn't say so, not now. He just sat there holding his untouched cup of coffee and looked at Winters from a smoothed-over, very blank face.

" He snuck in here, Dallas. It was just Frank's luck that he had to walk in on Sloan at the moment Sloan was untyin' that damned Circle S horse."

Dallas gently inclined his head. He kept watching Winters. " All right," he conceded quietly. " I'll go along with everything you've said so far, Curly. But what's next—that's what I want to hear from you."

Curly spread his hands out. " What is there to talk about Dallas? Sloan don't kill Frank Webster just like that, then ride back home and go to bed, does he?" Curly lifted his head and turned it to look around the room. The other DW men gravely nodded at him. Their minds, too, were made up on this score. Sloan—or whoever might have done that—wasn't going to escape his just punishment. Come hell or high water, those rangemen had their own code and it was inflexible. Law courts, fast horses, armed friends—none of those things was going to impede this killer's punishment.

Dallas lifted the cup, drank, set the cup down and quietly gazed over where Frank Webster's blanket-shrouded body lay. "He'll pay, Curly. He'll pay to the hilt. I reckon I should have shot him today when I had the chance. It just never occurred to me he'd do anything like this."

"He's no good," growled a Texan, "an' he never was no good."

Dallas drifted his sombre gaze around the lamplit, gloomy room. He was waiting for something. A lean, bronzed rider over at the stove re-filling his cup said in a soft drawl, "They been askin' for trouble ever since they hit the reservation gather. I say burn 'em out and shoot 'em on sight. Clean out the whole rotten nest of 'em, an' do it now—tonight."

A murmur of grim assent rose up after that statement. The man who'd said that turned, cup in hand, and gazed squarely at Dallas Wayne. The others also looked over at the table. They were ready now, and willing. In all their lamplit faces lay that ancient lust to fight, to kill and ravage.

Dallas finished his coffee, pushed the cup away and squared around on his bench. "One man did that. One man pays for it." The men began to mutter. Dallas said, "Wait a minute. I'll tell you what I think probably happened. Maybe Curly's already told you, maybe not, but Sloan and another Circle S man ambushed me over on Circle S range today. Shot the horse from under me."

Evidently Curly hadn't told the men, because now their expressions brightened with shock, with incredulity. They started to speak, to run a lot of astonished words

together in protest, in inquiry. Dallas shook his head at
them.

"Shut up and listen. We'll talk afterwards. I think
the reason Sloan came back for that horse tonight was
because he didn't want the people at Circle S to know
what he tried to do today. I think he particularly wanted
that bushwhack-attempt of his kept from Miss Smith. I
just can't imagine any other reason for him coming over
here like that. So, when you talk about attackin' all the
Circle S men, you're talkin' about shooting down men
over something I doubt like hell that more than one or
two even know about. Why else would Sloan run that
big risk just to get back his horse?"

The men pondered this. They sipped their coffee,
looked back and forth, looked over at Curly who usually
did their summing-up for them, and finally they watched
Dallas, saying nothing, just looking and waiting.

Curly broke the silence. He'd run all this through his
mind and it made sense to him, but the one thing upper-
most with him remained. He looked across the table,
saying quietly, "All right. Then it's just Ted Sloan—but
what do we do—sit here and wait for him to ride by?"

Dallas stood up, ignoring Curly's quiet sarcasm. "We
bury Frank," he said, "and after that, we do what comes
next."

They didn't ask him what came next. They simply
put aside their cups and milled a little, looked around at
one another. This burying business wasn't exactly new
to them but neither had any of them any clear-cut notion
of how it was to be done.

Dallas said: "Curly and I'll go dig the hole. You
fellers clean Frank up, slick down his hair and empty his
pockets into his war-bag. When we call, bring him out
wrapped in his bedroll." Dallas jerked his head at the

rangeboss, walked nearly to the door, then halted and looked mildly back with a puzzled expression. " Which of you know where Frank came from; how can we send his gatherings to his relatives?"

The others just shrugged or looked baffled, but Curly spoke as he started doorward. " Leave that to me. I know where he came from."

No one asked any question. Curly and Dallas left the bunkhouse, struck out across the yard for shovels and crowbars, silently took these utensils over near the main house, selected a likely spot and began to dig.

The ground was as yielding as iron, but at least they had the coolest time of night to work. In broad daylight this would have been a murderous chore. They didn't talk a whole lot for each in his own way was recalling little moments when their lives had touched the life of Frank Webster.

The night was paling off in the far-away east before Dallas climbed up out of the hole, flung down his shovel and mopped sweat off his face and neck. " Four feet deep," he said, " and six feet long."

Curly looked down into the hole. It was near the east end of the house where a locust tree grew. Each spring locust trees had big, cabbage-like fragrant flowers. Their petals, when they fell, were like soft blue snow.

" Nice spot. Frank'd think so too. Close by—nothin' can dig him up."

" Go over and give the boys a call," said Dallas, looking away from the grave. " Curly; when this is over I want to talk to you."

Winters was moving away. He stopped, looked around and said, " Yeah, I can guess what about. And that's odd, because Frank an' I—well—we talked about that other thing on the way back to the ranch today."

" What'd he say?"

" First he said he figured it was a damned lie. Then he said maybe it wasn't a lie, but he'd worked around you long enough to know you, an' if you—did that—you sure had a better reason than the mealy-mouths down around Virginia City say you had."

" Go call the boys, Curly."

Winters swung and walked away. He wasn't gone very long. When he returned the other DW men brought the body. Nothing was said as they eased Frank into the ground, but as they began rolling the dirt down upon him Dallas said a short prayer. After that they silently worked at filling the hole, at shaping it, tamping and moulding the earth. They seemed in no hurry at any of this but they *were* in a hurry and Dallas knew it.

He also knew something else. The moment he and his men showed up over in the Circle S yard at dawn, a battle was going to start unless he could devise some way of avoiding it, which, right this minute, seemed quite remote.

Curly straightened up at last, struck mouldy earth from his pants legs and said, " When we get back we can set about whittlin' up a headboard for Frank." He turned and looked straight at Dallas. The time had come to do what now remained to be done towards setting to rights the killing of their friend.

" Go saddle up," Dallas said, looking at them all. " I think we should let the book-law handle this, but I reckon you boys feel differently."

" We do," stated Curly Winters flatly. The others nodded and murmured assent with Curly's blunt statement. Dallas inclined his head. He only half-heartedly felt that the civil law should be called in. Actually, he wasn't any different from the others; his environment had taught him quite early that gun-law was best, swiftest, and most efficient and final.

"Then go saddle up."

The men began shuffling off towards the bunkhouse where their booted carbines hung, and then on down to the barn. All but Curly.

"You comin'?" he asked Dallas.

"Sure. Didn't you think I'd come?"

"Well. I reckon I did. Only just now when you said that about badge-law, I sort of got a feelin' you weren't really set on goin' over there."

"Curly; you and Frank talked about that story folks are passin' around about me. What do you think they'll say after we kill Sloan and ride roughshod over Circle S?"

"They'll say the right things, Dallas, when they know why we did this tonight."

"You sure of that? I'm not. You know what I think, Curly? I think this is a lousy world with a curse on it put there by men. People are a bunch of sand-fleas livin' in their own filth. They malign and kill and torture one another, most of the time without any reason. They breed in their own ignorance and their own stinkin' vice. They corrupt what started out clean an' decent. They aren't really honest, any of 'em; they don't know how to be honest. Someday a big wind'll blow out all the little lamps of men."

Curly said nothing. He looked at the grave, re-settled his hat and raised his eyes. Then, his gaze hard and practical, he said, "That all may be so, Dallas, but Frank's dead and the feller who killed him is still alive, and for my money some men are a heap worse than others, so we got to thin out the worst ones and maybe hope for the best from the others. You comin'?"

They walked on down across the cool, soft-lighted yard taking their time. At the bunkhouse Curly stepped in, stepped back out and handed Dallas a booted Winchester. " Frank's," he said, and they went along to where the other DW men were already saddling and bridling.

It was the shank of the night with pre-dawn chill strong in the air, with the heavens full of promise to man of better things than dust and sweat. There was a clarity to the atmosphere found nowhere else upon earth but in desert lands, and with it went an ageless fragrance of decaying things, of curing grasses on the stem, of sap running full in greasewood and sage and buckbrush. It was an old night, softened by nearing dawn but infinite in its agelessness; the best possible time to send one of God's insignificant little man-critters on his winging way. Much better to bury him in the solstice of the mysterious night than in the faded yellow glare of a working day.

There were six of them. One of them brought out Dallas's saddle, bridled horse and handed him the reins. They they swept up across the leather and looked at him. He turned, slackened the reins and rode around the barn, around the corrals, west-bound, and they strung out behind him, still not saying very much.

IT'S HARD, riding a vengeance-trail in the soft, pure night-time. A man thinks, and thought has a way of diluting resolve. Dallas went along out front with his reins swinging, with his feet loose in the stirrups, with his mind upon the things which live in every man's lonely heart, and by the time the Circle S buildings were distantly visible where new-day dawn-light struck tin roofs, he didn't feel the granite purpose he should have felt. He felt instead that somehow, Ted Sloan should first, have to stand up before everyone and explain why he'd killed Frank like that, without giving him his chance, then he should acknowledge what he deserved and be allowed to pay his penalty like a man.

But it wasn't going to be like that, Dallas knew. Curly and the other Texans with him were here to slay; they didn't believe a man had any right to his moment of final manhood for what Ted Sloan had done. Their code was harsh and barbaric. It was fair in its own way but it was also merciless.

A dog barked down among those buildings and a cowboy down at the barn strolled out into the pink, soft light to look up. He leaned upon his pitchfork to do this, but the moment he saw those bunched-up horsemen appear over a little ridge, pause briefly up there, then start walking their horses on down towards the yard, he hauled up stiff as a poker, staring hard.

This man might have had time to run to the bunk-house, run over to Burlette Smith's main house. But he didn't try. Probably because he was too stunned at what he saw, which was simply seven armed rangemen coming quietly down into the Circle S yard without making a sound, without hailing him which was the custom, or without even seeming to speak among themselves.

Then, by the time that astonished Circle S man made out the identity of the lanky, big man out front, it was too late; one of those DW riders had edged out a little to cut him off should he try to run. He didn't try; he simply stood there stiffly gawking.

A bristle-backed dog came prancing stiff-legged from around behind a shed. One of the DW men drew rein and told the dog to be quiet. He didn't snarl at the animal or even call him a name, which probably had much to do with the fact that the dog stopped his barking although he didn't lower his hackles as he slunk over closer to that familiar man holding to his pitchfork in front of the barn. The yard became quiet again. It was just breaking day.

Dallas gazed over at the bunkhouse. There was a little fluttery skiff of smoke rising from the tin stove-pipe over there. Someone was stirring the fire, probably putting the coffee pot on and getting ready to make breakfast. Dallas looked at Curly.

"Take two," he said, "and don't let them come bustin' out of there ready for war." Curly said two names and reined away. Dallas halted in front of the man at the barn's doorless opening, placed his hands atop the saddlehorn and leaned upon them gravely considering this rider.

" Where's Ted Sloan?" he quietly asked.

" Dunno," breathed the man, watching the other DW men come up and also halt, also sit up there looking gravely down at him. " What's wrong, Mister Wayne?"

" What do you mean you don't know where Sloan is? Isn't he in the bunkhouse?"

" No sir. When I got up an hour back to do the chores, his bunk was plumb empty—Mister Wayne."

From the bunkhouse came an angry squawk, then some sharp, low talk, and Curly appeared in the doorway. " Dallas—his bunk's empty. I don't think it's been slept in at all."

A screen door opened and slammed bringing men's faces quickly around towards the main house. Burlette was standing over there stiff and watchful. Under the veranda's roofline she appeared attired to ride but without a hat. Her red-auburn hair caught little flashes of the pinkish dawn light making it burn a steady dull copper.

" What do you want here?" she said, and although she hadn't raised her voice the words clearly carried. She was looking straight at Dallas Wayne. He turned his horse, walked it over to her and halted. He didn't dismount he simply leaned down slightly as he'd also done at the barn. They all heard his answer.

" I want Ted Sloan. Where is he?"

" In the bunkhouse, I suppose. Where else would he be? What are you doing over here like this—with all those armed men?"

" I came here to kill a man," Dallas said simply. " Maybe you knew Sloan shot a horse out from under me yesterday and maybe you didn't know that, but that's not what I want him for now. Last night he was in my barn after a Circle S horse, one of my riders walked in on him. Sloan killed him without a chance."

Burlette's face turned slowly grey. Her smoky eyes clung to Dallas's face. She put up a hand to her throat. Over at the bunkhouse a man squawked in angry protest again and another man growled a menacing curse at him, then that noise subsided and the only other sound in the yard was a horse snorting out back somewhere in a corral.

"I don't believe it," Burlette finally whispered. "I don't believe any of it. This is some more of your treachery, Dallas Wayne. You're trying in some underhanded way to strike back at me for stampeding your cattle."

"No ma'am. Stampedin' those cattle was a low trick, but then I've sort of come to the conclusion you're that kind of a person. But that didn't hurt me. It only inconvenienced my riders a little. What I just told you is the—"

"Hey Dallas," sang out Curly Winters from the bunkhouse doorway. "Look-a-here." Curly gave a half-dressed burly, hatless and bootless Circle S rider a fierce push out of the bunkhouse into the dusty yard. The man had a soiled wet rag across his upper face which he tugged at trying to free his eyes from its covering.

Curly walked down behind that man, stuck his pistol into his back and cocked it. The Circle S cowboy gasped and threw up both his heavy arms. "Don't," he cried frantically, wincing from that barrel-pressure. "Don't do it, mister!"

"Talk," ordered Winters. "And talk *loud*!"

Burlette stepped to the very edge of her porch. "Jake," she said. Then she turned on Dallas fiercely. "Can't you control your men? Don't you see that man is injured?"

Dallas didn't answer. He barely even looked at her. He said, " Go ahead, Jake—talk !"

" Is that you, Mister Wayne?"

" It's me, Jake."

" Don't let this feller shoot, Mister Wayne."

" Talk, Jake, and he won't shoot," replied Dallas, and gazed around at Burlette Smith. " Listen, ma'am. I think you're going to be interested in what Jake has to say."

Jake lowered his arms as Curly's pistol was taken out of his back. " It was Ted's notion—the whole thing. He said yesterday, when that lawyer-feller rode in sayin' he'd seen a rider comin' from the direction of DW, that we should go out there and put a scare into him. Mister Wayne, I swear it—that's all I figured we were goin' to do. I had no idea he'd shoot that horse from under you, then try to take you too. I swear to gawd I didn't."

" Go on, Jake," said Dallas. " All of it. Last night too. You were with him last night too, weren't you?"

" Yes sir. But all we was tryin' to do was get back that Circle S horse so's if you claimed we'd tried to shoot you we could deny it. I was out a ways holdin' the horses—honest to gawd I was, Mister Wayne. I don't know what'd happened until Ted come a-runnin'. He said some fool walked in just as he got the horse loose, and he'd had to shoot him. Mister Wayne . . .?"

Dallas turned away from Jake, put his level gaze upon Burlette Smith and waited. Jake started to whimper over there in front of the bunkhouse. Behind him upon the bunkhouse porch both Circle S and DW men stood without movement, gazing incredulously out at him. Curly reached forth, caught Jake's shoulder and coldly turned him, coldly prodded him back over to the shaded porch. The men moved back in total silence to let him go past, to go inside where the shade and the utter silence was most noticeable. He turned and made a pleading gesture with his hands but Curly Winters simply said, " Sit down, feller, an' if you know any prayers I sure advise you to say 'em."

Dallas kept watching the handsome girl. She'd been watching Jake like all the rest of them had been and now she stood there darkly in thought. Dawn pinkness glowed rustily through her hair, drew a circling pair of shadows across her breasts. She was breathing unevenly and after a while he saw revulsion cross her face, but it was gone in a second to be replaced by a dark wave of harshness. Her spirit was strong and wilful; whatever else she thought of her foreman and this Jake, and whoever else among her men might be close to those two, she was loyal.

She said, " I didn't know of any attack upon you yesterday, Mister Wayne, and I certainly had no inkling of a killing last night. But what do those things prove— that you have the right to kill also?"

" I reckon it does," he drawled down at her. He gently wagged his head. " You disappoint me, lady. I thought this might show you where the guilt lay. Instead you're stickin' up for them."

" I'm doing no such thing. I'm simply thinking that punishment isn't your responsibility, it's the law's."

" I see. And you're the judge," he murmured, closing his face to her.

She watched him, saw the black trouble in his eyes, saw the tough resolve and inherent discipline lying at the corners of his mouth making his lips a little flatter than was usual, saw the slight flare of his nostrils and the confident way his head sat atop his shoulders. She saw him as a handsome man with just the faintest hint of melancholy in his normal expression. He was the kind of a man who awakened in all women a slow, warm interest.

Slowly, coming down from her coldness a little, she said, "No, I'm not the judge, and neither are you." She turned, ran a glance across her Circle S men over by the bunkhouse. "Where is Ted?" she called.

The men shook their heads or stirred a little. One of them said, "Don't know, ma'am. Looks like his bed ain't been slept in."

Dallas said, "Curly? Get it out of Jake."

Curly disappeared from the bunkhouse doorway back inside. Over at the barn that rider leaning upon his pitchfork said into the lull and the stillness, "Ma'am; that big black gelding he rides mostly, ain't here, an' his outfit's gone too."

The DW men whispered briefly back and forth. It required very little imagination to understand their thinking now. If Ted Sloan was gone and his bunk hadn't been slept in, he'd unquestionably considered his predicament on the ride back after killing Frank Webster, and had decided that flight was his best chance for survival. Except for that, and also, as one of Dallas's men had formerly observed, excepting the fact that he'd taken back that Circle S horse from the DW barn, Sloan could have stood right there in their midst and brazened it out, because otherwise there was no proof that he'd killed Frank at all. A lot of suspicion, yes, but no actual proof, and these rangemen, angry as they were, would not have hung or shot him without proof.

Burlette said softly, "He was a fool."

Dallas chose to interpret this to mean she disapproved his fleeing but not his other acts. "I think he's your kind, ma'am, but just not as smart as you are." He started to turn his horse. They'd wasted enough time here. Wherever Sloan was they had to find him. The longer they delayed, the farther off he could get.

"Wait," she commanded. "You of all men, have no right to do this to Sloan. With your past what—?"

"Lady," said Dallas coldly, "Catch." He drew forth that oilskin little bundle he'd been carrying and tossed it to her. She caught it instinctively but stood with it in her outstretched hands perplexed and uncertain.

"Take it inside," he ordered. "Look it over. The next time we meet, give it back to me."

He whirled his horse, nodded at his men and started across the yard. Curly, in the bunkhouse doorway, called out to ask whether he hadn't better unload Circle S's guns. Dallas said it wasn't necessary and kept on riding. Curly went down to his horse and swung up. He and another DW man kept their eyes upon the unmoving Circle S riders as they rode away. They did this by sitting sideways in their saddles.

No one said anything until, halfway up that easterly rib of land with the full yellow brightness of daylight upon them, Dallas slowed to let the others crowd up.

"Where would he go?" he inquired of his men. Only two of them had any idea at all. One man suggested that he'd probably hide out until nightfall in order not to be seen upon the roundabout plains which would surely happen on a working day. Curly thought this was perhaps likely, but he said the most logical place for a fugitive to head for would be Virginia City. He also said Jake hadn't known anything.

"He'll need grub an' maybe more ammunition. He left Circle S in a rush. He wouldn't have had time to get that stuff at the ranch."

An experienced dry-country rider said, "He'll need a canteen full of water."

They began to swerve southeasterly towards Virginia City but Dallas had an idea that, although Sloan'd probably been in town, he wouldn't still be there. Not if he thought DW was riding in pursuit.

They were shuffling along through the building heat when Curly raised an arm. "Look yonder," he said, then heartily swore.

There was the rising dust of two horsemen speeding southward to get around them on the same route towards Virginia City. They were coming, significantly enough, from the northwestward direction of Circle S.

"Damn that woman anyway," a cowboy growled. "She knew all the time where he'd be."

Dallas wasn't ready to believe that, but he did believe Burlette had also concluded where Sloan might be, and had sent those two ahead to warn him.

" WE CAN head 'em off," Curly snapped, lifting his rein-hand waiting for the cue from Dallas. It came, along with a mutter of sharp profanity, and the race was on.

Those Circle S men had fresher horses but also, they were greatly out-numbered. Then too, although they were hastening right along, they were parallel to the DW riders.

For a while the race went on with neither side gaining. Dallas led his men on an angling course though, that promised, if all things remained equal, to cut across the front of Burlette Smith's men. He was clever at this; instead of driving straight for those two humped-over riders, he kept bearing steadily southeastward on a very long tangent which enabled him and his men to rush along nearly parallel with their prey while at the same time taking the longer view of eventually cutting across their front.

None of the men shouted or drew his guns or in any manner indicated open hostility towards another. They instead concentrated entirely upon riding hard and keeping it up.

Dallas's strategy eventually began to show how this race was going to end, though. He and Curly and one other DW man on a powerful horse, began to inch ahead on their diagonal course. Those Circle S riders saw this. They also, in desperation, saw that turning back would only put them at the mercy of the DW men on slower animals farther back. There was of course the alternative of abruptly wheeling to the right and racing away westerly, but this would only prolong a race they were now obviously going to lose anyway, and since there was nothing westerly for them but limited flight, they didn't offer to try this.

One of those men was a hundred feet ahead of the other. This man drew his sixgun. Instantly, off on his left and closing in fast, three other guns appeared. The Circle S man saw sunlight wickedly glinting off gun-steel and wisely returned his own gun to its holster. Then he slowly, grudgingly, began to haul back on his excited horse. The race was over, Circle S had lost.

Dallas flagged for a complete halt all around. Dust scuffed to life under the slowing horses. Those other DW men wheeled up and drew down. Both Burlette Smith's men scrupulously kept both their hands in plain sight. One bad move at a time like this, with excitement high, could bring quick death.

Both those men had been with Burlette the day DW had disarmed her escort beside her top-buggy. They had no reason at all to admire Dallas Wayne or his Texans. Their faces, flushed and wire-tight, were flinty towards their captors. Their eyes showed defiance, but they also showed defeat. It's hard for vanquished men to remain tough and wilful in the face of humiliation.

Dallas leaned upon his saddlehorn studying those two.

"Where is he?" Dallas asked, striking straight to the point. "She knew all the time, didn't she?"

The eldest of those Circle S riders shook his head. He was a whisker-stubbled, grizzled, hard-eyed man in his late thirties or early forties. He wasn't afraid of Dallas Wayne but he was respectful of him. " She don't know any more where Ted is than you do," he said firmly. " All she wanted to do was have us reach Virginia City before you did and warn the law what you fellers are up to."

Curly snorted at this, turned his head and spat dust. " Best time to run to the law," he growled, " is when you've done somethin' bad enough to need its protection. Anyway, mister, I think you're a liar."

The grizzled cowboy's eyes swivelled around, they were greeny eyes full now of quick malevolence. He nodded gently over at Winters. " You're safe callin' me that with all the guns on your side," he softly said. " But there'll be other times, friend. I'll remember that. I know who you are too. One time maybe we'll meet when the odds are a little evener. No man calls me a liar, mister. No man."

Dallas sat there pondering all this. He believed the Circle S cowboy. The reason he believed him was elemental. If Burlette had actually known where Sloan was hiding, had actually wished to protect him as Curly was convinced she did, it was inconceivable to Dallas that she'd have sent these two out so soon after DW had left Circle S, because she'd certainly have anticipated DW seeing and perhaps chasing them. On the other hand he thought her quite capable and willing to try and alert the law down in Virginia City. He wasn't convinced Burlette was on Sloan's side at all. He simply thought, as she'd implied back at the ranch, that she felt the duly accredited lawmen of Nevada should handle all this. That he *didn't* feel the same way only meant that he and she were poles apart in this matter, but then they were poles apart in most things.

"Someone's comin'," a DW cowboy said, pointing southward where dust was lifting behind a hastening buggy. "Looks like maybe they're comin' on from town."

The men craned around, all but Dallas who kept watching the Circle S men. "First things first," he admonished his men. "Curly, I think we'll take these two on down into town with us. That's where they seemed headed anyway." He cocked his head at the greeny-eyed Circle S man. "What's your name?"

"Harry Lyon."

"You want to keep your gun, Harry?"

Lyon shrugged. He wasn't sure of the meaning behind those words so he said nothing.

"I want your word you won't try using it on the way to Virginia City, Harry."

Harry sniffed. "I ain't that foolish, Mister Wayne. Like I told your rangeboss—the odds are too big. Me'n my pardner got nothing against livin'."

Curly suddenly swore. Dallas looked around. Winters was glaring out where a top-buggy was whipping up towards them. "That damned banker again," Curly grumbled, but he was only half right. There were two men in Stubblefield's rig. When George began to talk his horse down into a shuffling walk and lean on the lines, Dallas saw the second passenger in that buggy. He was a youngish man attired in the dark, rusty coat and trousers of a townsman and he had a slim leather valise of some kind lying upon his lap. He seemed as curious about big Dallas Wayne as the DW men on horseback seemed about him.

Stubblefield halted, looked quickly around and although no guns were showing, the banker seemed to sense this was no normal meeting of neighbouring cowboys who'd just happened to come together out on the range. He looped his reins around the buggy-whip and jack-knifed down out of the buggy. The thinnish, youngish man with the leather case on his lap kept staring up at Dallas without making any move to also alight.

Stubblefield put a bold face on this impromptu meeting and smiled up and down the line of unsmiling horsemen. He said to Dallas, " This here is Lawyer Billings, Dallas, the young man I've spoken to you about. Miss Burlette's attorney."

Dallas turned, eyed Billings in the buggy and gave him an almost unnoticeable nod. Billings nodded back. He looked into Curly Winters' grimly hostile countenance and into all those other yeasty glances. He still made no move to alight from Stubblefield's rig, but he said to Dallas, " Aren't those two men employees of Circle S ranch?" And nodded towards Lyon and the other cowboy.

" They are," Dallas said. " What about it?"

" Well. Perhaps nothing. Are you detaining them, Mister Wayne; I get the impression of a certain lack of neighbourly civility here and—"

Curly snorted so loudly it startled the lawyer. Another DW Texan broadly smiled. " Sure talks pretty don't he?" this man chuckled. " Neighbourly civility. Now you boys ever hear anythin' as musical as that before in your borned lives? Neighbourly civility. I got to remember that."

DW's men all smiled a little, even Curly Winters and big Dallas Wayne smiled. The lawyer turned brick red and the hand clasping that briefcase turned white at the knuckles. He looked slowly around, put aside the case and stepped out of the buggy. He was a lean, loosely put-together man perhaps no more than thirty-one or two, had reddish hair, a freckled nose and light blue eyes. He looked thin and boyish standing there. The only indication he wasn't altogether boyish was the tell-tale bulge of a holstered .45 under his coat. He looked straight at Curly and quietly said in a flat, Eastern accent, " Would you mind explaining what you meant to convey by that childish snort you just made."

Curly's eyes widened a trifle as he gazed down his nose at the lean, youthful man beside Stubblefield's buggy. He loosened in the saddle. " Say it plainer'n that, mister. I get the feelin' you're tryin' to pick a fight with me an' just plain don't know how to go about it."

George Stubblefield was standing beside Dallas's horse. He cleared his throat as though to intercede here but Dallas looked down, wagged his head, and Stubblefield wilted.

The lawyer thinly smiled. " For an ignorant cowboy," he said to Curly, enunciating very clearly. " You seem to have a fair grasp of English. Yes, that's exactly the intention I meant to convey. Would you care to dismount?"

Curly tumbled down out of his saddle and took three big forward steps before Dallas halted him. " Easy," Dallas said. " Curly, you're bein' baited."

Curly was mad now and flung a growl over his shoulder as he stalked ahead, shoulders hunched, fists up, head dropped down into a fold of one raised arm. " We'll damned soon see who's bein' baited. You fellers just mind them Circle S men while I trim the hide off this Yankee-talkin' dude here."

Dallas squared around. " Slack off," he said, with a hard snap to it. " We've got more important things to do, Curly; get back on your horse."

Winters hauled up short, glared at the attorney, glared up at Dallas, turned with a bitter oath and went back to his animal.

The lawyer stepped over closer to Dallas and without batting an eye said, " You're a wiser man than I thought, Mister Wayne. He wouldn't have had a chance."

Dallas considered Billings for a long, silent moment. There was something about him, something confident and graceful and seasoned, despite his youth. Dallas wondered if perhaps Curly mightn't have gotten the worst of it but he didn't say that, he in fact ignored this quick, threatening little interlude altogether and said, " Mister Billings, Stubblefield told me he'd mentioned my position to you about that ridiculous lawsuit."

" He did," stated the attorney. " Right now I'm on my way to Circle S to advise Miss Smith to press that suit for all she's worth."

" I see," murmured Dallas softly. " Let me tell you something, Billings—she's not worth enough. Not nearly enough. But if you're dead-set on breakin' her by dragging that silly thing into court, she'll probably go along with you. Not because she figures she'll win those big damages, not because she hates my guts. And you— well—you'll come out smellin' of roses. Your fee's not concerned with win, lose or draw, is it?"

Billings didn't drop his eyes for Dallas any more than he had for Curly Winters. He seemed to be a brave man or a foolish one, and thus far no one could definitely say which. " She's got a good case, Mister Wayne."

" Yeah? Ten thousand dollars worth?"

" A law court will decide that."

" Sure. And she won't get back half her lawyer's fees. A court'll decide that too, won't it?"

Billings shifted his position. He said, " Why are you

so interested in trying to save her money for her, Mister Wayne?"

Dallas didn't answer that. He sat perfectly still gazing downwards. Why *was* he? Curly and the other DW men also gazed at Billings, slow doubt and wonderment coming into their faces. Billings had made a point.

Dallas shifted in the saddle, looked at his men and nodded. "Let's get along," he murmured. At his knee George Stubblefield spoke up swiftly, seeking a delay in DW's departure.

"Dallas; what's wrong this time? Where were you men going when we came up?"

"After a murderer," answered Dallas, and reined away.

Stubblefield was stunned. Even the lawyer's poise slipped. Both of them spoke out, but the horsemen were going past with their Circle S captives. They scarcely even bothered to drop a glance upon men afoot.

Heat was now a physical thing; it had been steadily piling up all through that meeting back there. It pushed downward across the riders' shoulders, it punished them with its breathlessness, it hazed the onward world into a blurry mirage that constantly wavered and writhed.

They had a number of miles yet to go. Their Circle S companions were sullenly silent and grim-faced. They went along without offering trouble but there was not one shred of doubt, from the looks of them, that the moment they were free of DW they were going to complain shrilly of being forced along like this.

Curly Winters, long silent and thoughtful, eventually eased up beside Dallas to ask a question which was deeply troubling him.

"You reckon that Yankee-feller couldn't have whupped me, Dallas?"

Wayne shrugged. He didn't know, hadn't thought much about it, and didn't really care. " I think he knows something about himself we don't know, Curly."

" But hell; he's a skinny, pasty-lookin' outfit if I ever saw one."

Dallas swung his head. He slowly smiled. Curly was having his doubts. That lawyer had the Indian-sign on him. " The way you're feelin'," Dallas said, " he could beat you to death with a feather right now, Curly. No man ever won a fight when he secretly didn't think he could."

Winters bristled, touched on a raw spot. " Wait until the next time. I'll show you. And Dallas—next time don't haul me off. All right?"

" Sure, all right, Curly."

Dallas looked ahead. Virginia City was rising up off the flat plain, dancing in the midday heat. There was a tan, tawny, dusty mistiness hanging over the place like there always was in summer time. Virginia City was a thriving, bustling town.

14

BEN WILLETT was town constable, and while the authority of constables ordinarily ended at the town limits, Virginia City like many other towns west of the Missouri with miles of emptiness all around and limited law enforcement facilities, had long ago petitioned the county and territorial agencies to deputise its town constable so that he could also exercise his duties countywide.

Ben was an affable middle-aged man who was fast enough with a gun but more than that, he was quick-witted, and because of this Ben had been able to out-think more wild range-riders, outlaws and sharpers, than he'd ever had to out-shoot.

He was in the Green Door Saloon having a lukewarm stein of beer when George Stubblefield came bustling in all red and sweaty, his necktie askew, his shoulders covered with trail-dust. Phil Billings was with George, but Billings was a lot less ruffled.

"Ben," croaked Stubblefield, his agitated manner and appearance making him the focal point of everyone in the saloon which included perhaps ten or fifteen loafing rangemen and perhaps an equal number of townsmen. "Ben, listen to me. Dallas Wayne's on his way here with six of his Texans. They've got a pair of Circle S men captives. Mister Billings an' I talked to them not more'n twenty minutes ago. Dallas said there'd been a murder and he's out after the murderer. You've got to do—"

" Easy, George," said the lawman, gazing with mild disapproval upon Stubblefield. " Let's have the first part of that again. Dallas Wayne told you there'd been a murder?"

" Yes," gasped Stubblefield. " Don't take my word for it, ask lawyer Billings here."

Ben Willett gazed dispassionately at Billings and back to the banker again. " I'll take your word," he said, beginning to look irritated. " It's good enough, George. Hell man—get hold of yourself. Now then, who's been murdered and who does Dallas think done it?"

" He didn't say. Listen, Ben, he'll be riding into town any time now. You've got to get out there and stop him."

" Why?" asked Willett. " He's not after you is he— or me—or this here lawyer-feller? George, you're makin' a spectacle of yourself. I tell you again—get hold of yourself."

Willett slowly lifted his gaze from Stubblefield, glanced around the hushed room where some twenty or thirty men were watching and listening, and gently shook his head. He came back to studying Billings. He knew who the lawyer was. He also knew why he was in Virginia City, and primarily because Ben Willett had very little use for lawyers, when he addressed the attorney, his tone of voice was dry and crisp.

" What's this all about, Mister Billings?"

" Just exactly what Mister Stubblefield has told you, Constable. We met Wayne and his crew out on the range. They'd evidently just come from Circle S and had two Circle S men with them, as hostages I believe."

" I see. An' did those Circle S men have guns on, Mister Billings?"

" Well; yes they did have, but—"

" No buts, Mister Billings. You ever hear of anyone havin' armed hostages with 'em?"

Billings' eyes narrowed in frank hostility. " Constable, the details are not what counts now. As Stubblefield said, you've got to stop those Texans."

" All right," agreed Willett agreeably. " I'll stop 'em. But what am I stoppin' them from, mind explainin' that to me?"

" You've been told, Constable. Wayne is after someone he believes is a murderer. When he rides into town ask him. I doubt if he'll tell you. He doesn't impress me as a very rational or law-abiding man."

Ben Willett raised his bushy, grey eyebrows slightly. " Don't he? Well, that's strange, Mister Billings. Dallas Wayne's only been hereabouts some four or five years, an' already he owns his DW outfit, several buildings here in town, and has the loan-papers on half a dozen local businesses. I'd say that's a pretty good record for an irrational, un-law-abidin' man, wouldn't you?"

Over against a shadowy rear wall of the saloon an old, battered rancher with his hat tilted back and his chair tipped up, said to Phil Billings, " Mister; why don't you keep your long nose out of local affairs? I been around here twenty years an' I've never seen a time when local folk couldn't handle anythin' that come up."

Billings twisted to seek out that speaker. He and the cowman locked hard, hostile glances. Billings said, " I've been brought here to prosecute Dallas Wayne and I mean to—"

" Naw," interrupted the old cowman, " The man you

want is named Brannan. He's the one that cut Miz' Smith's trees down, not Dallas Wayne."

"Wayne is responsible under the law. He—"

"Mister," drawled the cowman. "You been listenin' to loose talk, an' bein' a fee-lawyer an' all, you sort of smelt a chance to eat up hearty, like a buzzard."

Billings, stung by the growing hostility towards him in the faces along the bar, at the poker tables, back over where that tough old cowman lounged, said sarcastically, "Now tell me you haven't heard some other unsavoury stories about Dallas Wayne, gentlemen. Tell me you—"

A loose-standing, younger man at the bar who'd been paring his fingernails with a wicked-bladed knife snapped the thing closed with finality, raised his head and interrupted Billings, and this man's drawl was pure Texas as he said, "Yankee, if I was in your boots I'd mind my tongue a little."

Billings' breath ran out in a long hiss as he faced the direction of this fresh challenge. Somehow, whatever these men privately thought of Big Dallas Wayne, regardless of their special and private suspicions or judgements of him, Billings, the hostile stranger in their midst, had made his very poor first impression and they were openly antagonistic towards him. He saw this, thought about it, looked away from that sultry-eyed young cowboy at the bar back towards Stubblefield, and said in a tone meant to be both belittling and scornful, "Let's go down to the bank, Mister Stubblefield. It was a pure waste of time pushing your horse as hard as we did to arrive here in town ahead of Wayne and his bunch of drifters."

Stubblefield, mopping his face with a limp handkerchief, looked appealing up at Constable Ben Willett.

" He'll be riding in, Ben. Stop him. I'm not saying he's altogether wrong, all I'm asking is that you stop him before there's a real war between DW and Circle S."

Willett solemnly nodded down at the banker. " I'll talk to him," he said, and after gazing a moment into Stubble-field's anxious countenance, he said in the same quiet way, "You need a drink, George. Can I buy you one?"

Stubblefield shook his head, turned and joined Phil Billings in hiking out of the saloon. For a moment after the departure of those two no one spoke, but gradually there rose up a murmur of interest, as men discussed the things which had been said. That youthful cowboy at the bar sidled down beside Ben Willett, flagged for a beer and hooked his elbows over wood as he quietly gazed upon the constable.

" What you aim t'do, Constable?" he drawlingly asked. " Them two worry-warts struck me as gen-u-ine trouble-makers."

Willett cooled the cowboy. " What I do is my business, cowboy. Your business seems to be drinkin' beer."

Willett walked on out of the saloon.

Behind him several little groups of men got up and sauntered over to the spindle-doors, paused there to mumble a little back and forth, then pushed on out into the afternoon brightness and leaching heat. Some of them walked southwards, some walked northward. There were recessed doorways, benches, shaded places the full length of Virginia City's main thoroughfare where curious onlookers could sit and wait. It was a dull, hot afternoon; any promise of action was better than endlessly loafing in the Green Door drinking lukewarm beer.

Ben Willett went down to his office, took a short-barrelled-scattergun from his wall rack, hooked the weapon casually over his elbow and strolled back outside. It was always something; seemed as though a man just never could entirely relax during the hot months. He stood a moment out front gazing across at Stubblefield's bank building. Slanting sunshine was hitting harshly against those yonder windows so he couldn't see into George's office, but he was confident Stubblefield would be in there. Anyway, he wasn't as interested in the banker as he was in the lawyer-feller Miss Burlette had imported. That one, in Ben Willett's knowledgeable opinion, was a trouble-maker. Ben stepped to the plankwalk's edge, spat and stepped back again. There was a time when trouble came to Virginia City riding a big horse and wearing a tied-down gun, which was, in Ben Willett's opinion, the way trouble should always appear. Not packing a leather briefcase and wearing a frock coat like a cussed preacher or undertaker.

Still, Ben got that same impression about Billings that Dallas Wayne had also gotten. There was more to this youthful, clear-eyed, crisp and confident attorney than showed on the surface. He wore a gun under his coat, which at least lifted Billings out of the pilgrim class, but it wasn't altogether that. Ben couldn't define it any more than Dallas had been able to. The difference here was that while Ben stood in the shade out front of his jailhouse he had nothing else to do but ponder it, while Dallas Wayne, approaching Virginia City from the heat-blurred north, didn't try to fathom it. Dallas was preoccupied with where he was going to find Ted Sloan.

He was reasonably certain Sloan wouldn't still be in Virginia City. Too much time had elapsed since the killing of Frank Webster. But he was just as confident that Sloan had been there, and this is what kept him going now; someone in town would have seen Sloan, would have perhaps sold him supplies, and in all probability, would have noticed which direction he'd ridden when he left town.

He'd seen Stubblefield and Billings whip up the banker's horse and go wheeling frantically on towards town. When his men urged him to overtake them, to prevent them from getting into Virginia City to spread the alarm and perhaps even flush Ted Sloan out and warn him, Dallas had ignored that to give an entirely different set of orders.

He knew Stubblefield would go directly to Constable Willett. He also knew the kind of man Willett was, so he said, " Curly; we're going to split up right here. Now you boys listen. I think Sloan hit town, got supplies and probably ran on. We're going to break up here; you fellers ride in pairs, go out and around Virginia City and stop at ranches, at freighter-camps, any place you see men, and you ask if anyone has seen Sloan, or someone who resembles him, go past. Then you all head on southward and after I'm through quieting down Ben Willett an' anyone else Stubblefield and Billings have got worked up against me, I'll ride on south—alone—an' you fellers keep an eye peeled so's we can all come together again below town."

The riders nodded and looked at one another to pair off. Curly Winters though, frowned. " Suppose they don't let you leave town?" he asked. " An' what about these Circle S prisoners?"

" How can they stop me?" countered Dallas. " We haven't done anything. The main thing is—we don't want Ben Willett an' a town-posse interfering. That's what I aim to prevent happening. Now let's split up. You Circle S men—go on, ride off."

The men reined off in pairs. Curly, still reluctant to

depart from Dallas, still full of dark doubts about this strategy, finally rode away darkly frowning.

Virginia City was close enough to Dallas for him to clearly make out its roadway traffic, which was lightest during the heat of the day, and also the unusual number of riders passing into and out of, town. As he rode on it struck him that Sloan, who'd been foreman of Circle S for more years than Dallas himself had been in this country, probably had friends among the cowmen. It also struck him that, since that war-time story was common knowledge now, that he himself probably had enemies now that he hadn't had before, and whom he didn't even know were his enemies. Since the scars of war healed slowly and prejudice died hard in this or any other predominantly Yankee-Union countryside, he approached Virginia City with a sense of resentment, of bitterness, colouring his thoughts.

Just before he entered town by the way of the northward road he wondered whether or not the fact that he was now a controversial personality, might not actually be Ted Sloan's greatest asset. He saw loafing men lined up along the roadway on both sides watching him. He also saw how these men, who very obviously knew why he was now in town, kept craning around as though seeking other men they plainly thought should be riding with him. He let his bronzed features turn ironic. Stubblefield and Billings had done their work well in Virginia City.

Half way down the thoroughfare Ben Willett stepped down into roadway dust from the shaded place in front of his jailhouse. Ben had a shotgun cradled across his left arm for sudden action, which made Dallas's irony turn more deeply noticeable across his face.

People watched from doorways, from windows and

benches lining the roadway as those two came together. They strained to hear what was said, but none succeeded for both Wayne and Constable Willett were soft-spoken men.

"Hello, Dallas. You come alone, did you?"

"Howdy, Ben. Don't see anyone with me do you?"

Willett didn't bother glancing farther back. His look was amiable, was relaxed while at the same time it was also resolute. "Dallas; George Stubblefield and that lawyer-feller said there'd been a murder an' you were out after the killer. What about that?"

"Ted Sloan slipped into my barn last night, Ben, and killed Frank Webster."

"Why?" asked Willett quietly.

Dallas leaned across his saddlehorn and recited all that had happened to him within the last two days. Willett listened, grounded his scattergun had leaned upon it with sweat dappling his face. He never once removed his eyes from Wayne's face, but when Dallas was finished speaking Willett gently waggled his head back and forth.

"All right, Dallas. Until I hear the other side I'll accept your version. Not that I don't believe you, mind; only every dog's entitled to his day. But you can't take the law into your own hands. You know that. You're no hair-brained range-rider who races off half-cocked."

Dallas pondered the constable's craggy, oily features. He'd known Willett four years and liked him. "Ben; I didn't say I was dead-set on lynchin' Sloan."

"Just shootin' him," muttered the constable dryly.

"Nor that either, unless he makes me do it, Ben. I aim to catch him first, then fetch him back to town for folks to condemn and hang."

Willett inclined his head, staring straight up into

Dallas's face. " All right," he murmured. " An' where are your men right now? Out lookin' for Sloan, an' when they find him—if they do—are you goin' to sit up there an' tell me those Texans of yours are goin' to meekly bring him back to Virginia City?"

" Ben, if I'm with 'em when they find him that's exactly what they'll do."

" What d'you mean—if you're with them?"

Dallas nodded downwards at Willett's shotgun. " Did you figure to detain me with that thing, Ben?"

Willett looked down then upwards again. He didn't answer back right away. Northward up the roadway there was a distant beat of bunched-up riders swiftly approaching. He craned outwards to see around Dallas's horse. Dallas also turned to see what this meant. He saw. So did Constable Willett. Ben blew out a big sigh and sealed it with a mild curse.

" Circle S with Miz' Smith leadin', Hell's bells, Dallas, why do these things always have to happen on hot days?"

15

THIS WAS something Dallas hadn't expected although perhaps he should have. As Burlette slowed her horse the men riding with her also slowed. Over in front of the Green Door stood Harry Lyon and that other Circle S rider Dallas had brought almost into town with him. They stood and gravely watched their employer and their riding companions pass by without stepping out to go to them, or without even waving or lifting their hats at Burlette. This, Dallas noticed.

"Well," growled Ben Willett, "get off your horse, Dallas, and come on over to the office. Miz' Burlette's got blood in her eye too, it appears like." The constable turned and stalked back over into jailhouse shade.

Dallas considered Burlette as she approached. She'd seen him of course, and now didn't look left or right, but kept her cold, hostile gaze steadily upon him. He saw her expression but he also saw how she sat her saddle, how she handled her horse with a light, left-handed touch, and he admired her; disliked her but at the same time admired her.

He turned, reined on over to the rack in front of Ben's jailhouse, swung out and down, stepped over, wrapped his reins and moved on up into the shade with

Constable Willett. When Burlette came up and halted, her riders were grim-faced and tough-eyed around her. Constable Willett asked her to also alight. She was beginning to, when over at the bank a door opened and Phil Billings stepped through. He'd obviously sighted Burlette from Stubblefield's office window. He started on over.

Willett's expression of distaste and resignation got longer but he turned, pushed his office door inward and stepped aside. Burlette entered first. She had to step squarely in front of Dallas Wayne to do this; she didn't look up or even act as though she were aware he was anywhere around. Out in the road the Circle S swung down. Ben turned and shook his head at them. " Go have a drink," he ordered. " You won't be needed here."

Billings pushed through to say, gazing straight at Dallas, " Maybe they will be needed, Constable."

Willett, catching this innuendo and in no mood for it, flared out at the lawyer. " Mister; you better mind your tongue. I've had about all of you I can stomach. Now if you're comin' in here you mind your cussed manners or out you go !"

Dallas entered the office, Billings came in behind him, and the last man in was Ben Willett himself. He closed the door, removed his hat, tossed it upon a littered desk and roughly indicated with an outflung arm that everyone should be seated.

At once the lawyer spoke up. " This is not an official interrogation, I take it, Constable, and therefore nothing which is said here by my client can be considered admissive or binding."

Willett sat down, leaned back in his desk-chair and gazed at Billings for almost thirty seconds without speaking a word. Evidently, when Ben had said outside he'd had just about all he could stomach, he hadn't been speaking loosely.

Dallas watched Burlette and she, in turn, sat very stiffly, very defiantly, never once even casually glancing in his direction. When Willett began questioning her she offered every answer truthfully and briefly, but there was really very little that she knew beyond the fact that the DW men had come unexpectedly into her yard earlier this same day seeking her foreman.

"Mister Wayne said Sloan had killed one of his riders, but I know nothing about that at all. I have only his word about it, Constable."

Ben said gravely, "Do you figure Dallas Wayne is lyin', ma'am?"

Billings broke in. "She's already told you she didn't see any killing and has only hearsay to go by, Constable."

Ben looked quietly at Billings again and still didn't speak to him. He shifted his attention to Dallas. "Did you explain to Miz' Smith how that shootin' came about, Dallas?"

"I did. When we met at her place this morning I told her everything."

Billings broke in again, but before he'd completed a single sentence the constable cut him off with a plaintive-sounding question. "Mister Billings—how old are you?"

"What? What possible business can that be of yours, Constable? What bearing can it have on . . .?"

"Well, I'll tell you, Mister Billings. I'm crowding fifty, and for thirty years I've been a lawman of one kind or another. In those thirty years I've learned my share of book-law. Now then—in my office, in my town, among my friends, you're just about the last feller on this earth I aim to put up with always interruptin' and makin' a plumb nuisance of yourself. So be a nice lad; just sit over there and shut up, will you?"

Billings sprang out of his chair. Dallas looked over at him, saw the danger signals in Billings' face and eyes, and softly spoke. " Easy, friend. Step real easy. I'm goin' to also give you a piece of advice. Don't brush back that coat and don't take a step. You'd never complete either of them."

Billings' nostrils flared as he swung his head towards Dallas Wayne. " If you're threatening me," he said softly, " I'll give you a chance to back it up—even a cold-blooded throat-cutter like you is entitled to his even break."

It was the wrong statement from the wrong man. Dallas exploded out of that chair in a lunging blur. Even Ben Willett who knew Dallas as well as anyone in Virginia City, had no idea so large as man could move so fast.

But Phil Billings showed now what it was that both Wayne and Willett had felt about him and which they had both been unable to define. He whipped forward onto the balls of his feet, stepped clear of Dallas's rush, lashed out with a bony fist and cracked Dallas under the left ear.

Constable Willett jumped out of his chair. Even Burlette sprang up, but she stood tensely watching without moving an inch while the constable growled and moved towards the lawyer. That was a mistake; Ben should have drawn his gun to stop this fight. He didn't, probably because he imagined himself a match for any spindle-shanked young whippersnapper out of some eastern law school, and that was Ben's big miscalculation. Billings spun around, glided forward on the balls of his feet and caught Ben flush on the point of the chin as he was coming in. Ben crumpled without a sound and fell in a heap near Burlette Smith's feet. She bit her under-lip and stared.

Dallas balanced there watching Billings. He knew now what he was up against; a trained fist-fighter. He made a craggy little smile with his lips recalling Curly's doubts about this same man. He also had some doubts. He'd fought with guns and knives and fists, but never for the sake of fighting, and he therefore was not schooled as a fighter. And yet, having survived his share of fights to the death, had learned for himself a few elemental facts about preservation and attack. He used one of them now; he circled counter-clockwise to force Billings off-balance, to force his adversary to constantly shift position to meet him. Billings smiled a cold, merciless small smile. " Good thinking," he murmured, ignoring everything in the office except Dallas Wayne. " But then you'd be a calm thinker anyway, wouldn't you Wayne? A man who'd deliberately kill an unarmed prisoner of war to insure his own profiteering would be a calm thinker."

The obvious purpose behind that statement wasn't lost on Dallas. He resented that statement exactly as he was supposed to, but he did not furiously charge Billings, which he was also supposed to do. He instead danced in, flicked outward with a little jab which Billings sucked clear of, then he feinted, attempting to draw the lawyer to him.

Billings didn't come in, though. He simply kept turn-ing and grinning, his hands half way up, fisted and riding easily with each graceful turn of the lighter man's body. " Try something original," he murmured to Dallas. " Like using your hidden Bowie knife, Mister Wayne."

Burlette stepped forward with her face as pale as death, with her wintry grey eyes nearly black. " You

have no right to say these things," she said to Billings.
" No right at all."

Billings didn't look around. He didn't even lose his
little smile. He simply retorted to Burlette in that same
soft and murmuring, that same taunting voice of his.

" Lady; keep out of this. I came here to get you ten
thousand dollars and I'll get it from this murdering thief
if I have to beat him bloody to do it. Just stand back
and remember our agreement—we split half and half."

That was the first inkling Dallas had that Burlette
wasn't going to have to pay Billings cash for pushing her
lawsuit against him. He'd heard of contingency-fees before, but since such arrangements were considered highly
unethical by frontier lawyers, it hadn't once occurred to
him that Burlette Smith would be involved in such an
affair. He glanced at her as he and Billings kept circling,
kept pawing at one another seeking an opening, and saw
her sudden swift colouring. As he sidled past he said,
" You're as rotten as I thought you were, aren't you? I
half doubted that when I decided to let you know what
happened back there at Sabine Pass during the war. I
thought you might be the kind of a woman I see now
you're not. Do like Billings says—keep out of the way."

Burlette retreated as far as where Ben Willett was beginning to moan softly and stir feebly on the floor. She
dropped swiftly beside the constable, lifted his head and
began to frantically work at bringing Willett around.

Dallas took two stinging blows alongside the head and
another harder blow in the chest. He made no attempt
to sidestep these punches for an excellent reason. He was
no longer circling Billings now, he was instead
manoeuvring him backwards towards a corner of the
office. He knew he couldn't hope to out-box Billings. He
also knew if he rushed in again he was going to be badly

cut by those experienced hard fists. But he also knew that if he could keep Billings too occupied to realise that he was being put into the corner, he might then be able to weather the fistfighter's best strikes, and that his own greater power and heft would give him an even chance at winning this fight.

He swung a looping strike calculated to miss narrowly, and it did because Billings rocked back from it. He threw three rapid, vicious little jabs. One connected, the other two pawed empty air again. He ducked under a lightning blow and hit Billings in the mid-section driving him still further back. Then, with his shoulders only inches from the wall, Billings suddenly understood what had happened and tried a quick sidestep. Dallas was there to block him. Billings drew back, half-turned to jump the other way, and Dallas saw his opening while the seasoned fist-fighter had this other thing to concentrate upon. He whipped in with both fists pumping. He caught Billings along the ribs, spinning him further away. He struck him across the chest as Billings was rocking forward and this time the lawyer's back hit the wall.

Dallas ducked away from a flashing left and ran head-on into a blasting right. He blinked as Billings turned blurry in his sight, bored ahead and hit the lawyer twice, a right and a left, in the soft parts. Billings' breath exploded outward. Dallas tasted the salty oiliness of blood inside his mouth but the punishing jab that had struck his face glancingly causing that taste had no pain connected to it for him. He was fighting on will alone now, was aiming by instinct. He caught Billings bouncing off the wall with a chopping overhand blow that drove the attorney back into the wall again. He hit him with his body fully twisting in behind the blow, flush over the heart. He saw Billings' head snap forward, saw his light hair fly wildly from impact. He set both legs wide and worked the attorney's upper body, dropped down and punished his middle, stepped back one foot and with clearing sight, dropped his right shoulder, dropped his right fist, set himself and threw a crushing right fist that cracked like a pistol-shot against the lawyer's jaw.

Billings's head banged off the rearward wall. His eyes turned up and his mouth sagged. He sagged ahead into Dallas nearly carrying them both to the floor. Dallas caught hold, pushed the attorney off, twisted sideways and let Billings go down all in a heap.

He put out a hand to brace himself upon the wall, gazed downward and sucked in enormous amounts of whistling breath. He had beaten the experienced fist-fighter.

Ben Willett said thickly, " Good. Here, Miz' Smith, help me up."

Burlette got Ben unsteadily up onto his feet. He ran an explorative set of fingers over his bruised jaw. He glared at the unconscious lawyer and turned to reach for his chair.

" Get Dallas a pitcher of water and a towel," he said roughly to Burlette. " Then I think I'll lock both you an' your bully-boy up for a few days. Go on; get that damned water an' towel, girl, don't just stand there lookin' like someone just yanked the world out from under you."

There was a small washstand across the office and as Burlette went over to it, Dallas straightened off the wall, half turned and said, " Ben; I've got some ridin' to do. You got any objections?"

Willett started to shake his head. He was still exploring his swollen jaw and darkly, thunderously scowling.

"You're damned right I got objections," he thickly stated. "We'll *both* go ridin', Dallas. Only first off, you wash up, then give me a hand draggin' this bag of carrion into a cell."

Burlette came over with the pitcher and basin. She looked squarely up at Dallas Wayne. "I want you to know something," she said. "That wasn't true, what he said about dividing the damages I collected from you. He came out to the ranch yesterday with that proposition. I told him I wouldn't have any part of it. Then he told me that you'd offered to buy him off, through George Stubblefield, and that if I didn't accept his proposition, he'd accept the offer you'd made to buy him off. I fired him, Mister Wayne; told him that if you and he fought like that, I wouldn't soil myself by having anything to do with either of you. I told him to forget the lawsuit; that I'd forget it too. That I'd find some other way to humble you."

Dallas bent forward, ran both bruised hands into the basin of water, sluiced off his face and tenderly felt his battered mouth where the cool water stung. He didn't say anything, didn't even look at her when he picked up the towel and began dabbing at his raw face with it, and when he was finished he looked over at Willett and said, "You ready to ride, Ben, because if you aren't I'm going without you."

"Sure I'm ready. Give me a hand lockin' these two up first," growled Willett, standing up to test his rubbery legs.

16

THEY LEFT Virginia City riding side by side and heading southward. Dallas explained to Ben Willett why they were heading in that direction and old Ben grumpily nodded, saying, " I knew all along you had your crew with you somewhere hereabouts. Stubblefield and that lawyer-feller came bustin' into the Green Door an hour ago to warn me."

" That lawyer," mused Dallas as they rode along, " is a damned fool. An opportunist who probably functions well enough in his own environment—wherever that is—but who does all the wrong things out here in Nevada."

" T'hell with him," growled the constable. " I'll take care of him when I get back. And *her* too, for that matter. Hirin' a feller like that, stirrin' up all this trouble in the middle of summer, gettin' folks shot an' shot at. Hmph!"

They were clearing the southernmost environs of Virginia City when Dallas said, " Ben, go easy on her. She had her reasons. Maybe not very good reasons, but she thought they were. Anyway, she's a woman—and women don't reason like a man does."

" They sure don't," agreed Ben Willett forcefully. " They don't reason at all, they just rationalise with emotion, which is about like sayin' they think with their hearts an' feelings."

"Ben; she'd heard that story about me at Sabine Pass."

Willett, his mouth open to speak, suddenly fell silent and turned to gaze across at Dallas. He appeared to want to ask a question, to thresh out something which had evidently been in his mind for a long time. But Ben was a discreet man as well as a shrewd one, so all he ultimately said in a subdued way was: "Look yonder; a rider high-tailin' it out of town ahead of us. Now who the hell'd be in such a hurry on a hot afternoon?"

Dallas picked up that racing rider's dust and followed it on ahead to the horse which was making it. He sat silent and alert for a long time. He seemed to be waiting for something. That onward man raced away at a swift pace, got small in the yellow-burning distance until even his dust-banner became diffused in the flat light, then from both sides of the roadway riders jumped their horses out, closed in and halted the racing horseman. Dallas relaxed, turned and flintily smiled.

"We'll find out who he is and what his hurry is. Those are my men who just stopped him."

Ben squinted ahead and nodded to himself. He'd anticipated such a meeting, but not entirely like this; not with the DW riders holding someone hostage down there. As Willett eased back, content to mosey along leisurely beside Dallas Wayne, he said, "You don't reckon that was Circle S's foreman they caught do you, Dallas?"

Wayne shook his head still looking far ahead down the dusty roadway. "If that'd been Sloan they wouldn't have taken him without a fight. This feller just saw my boys and quit."

Down where those horsemen were milling around their captive someone evidently saw Dallas and his companion approaching, for one man turned and slow-loped on up towards them. When he was still a considerable distance off Dallas recognised him.

"Curly Winters, my rangeboss," he said to Constable Willett. They halted to let Curly lope right on up, and when Winters threw them a little wave, they waved back.

Curly halted up close, gazed at Willett and waited for Dallas to say something, which Dallas did by explaining that Constable Willett was going to ride with them in their pursuit of Frank Webster's killer. Curly listened and nodded, but his eyes mutely told Dallas he didn't approve of this at all. Then he said, "We got a friend of yours down there, Dallas. He came a-foggin' it along like a band of warwhoops were behind him. Stubblefield, the banker."

Dallas was surprised and showed it. So was Ben Willett. Ben curled his forehead and puckered his brows. "George Stubblefield? What in the name of the devil would George be doin' ridin' like that in the heat of the day?"

Curly regarded Willett a moment in silence, then reached inside his shirt, drew out a brown-wrapped packet with one corner recently torn open, and tossed it casually across to the constable.

"Maybe that'll give you some notion," he dryly said.

Willett looped his reins as Dallas bent sidewards to also see what was inside the packet. Ben tore at that corner and let his breath out explosively. "Money! There must be six, eight hundred dollars in here," he said, holding the bundle out so Dallas could also see the crisp sheaf of bills.

Curly smiled. " More'n that, Constable. There's an even thousand. We already counted it."

" Stealin' from his own bank?" murmured Ben Willett, looking up and around. " But why?"

Dallas's surprise faded fast to be replaced by a thoughtful expression and a speculative glance at Curly Winters. " What did he say about the money?" he asked.

" That he was deliverin' it to a rancher south of town."

Dallas slowly shook his head at Winters. " Know what I'm thinkin'?" he asked quietly, and Curly nodded firmly and immediately.

" Sure. The same thing I thought when we first found that money on him. Rancher hell—*he's takin' that money to Ted Sloan.*"

Constable Willett stiffened in his saddle. He looked sharply towards Winters, then just as sharply over at Dallas Wayne. " No," he said, in a low, doubting voice. " Why would George Stubblefield do a thing like that? Hell; where would there be any connection between George an' Sloan?"

Dallas lifted his rein-hand and kneed out his horse. " I know one pretty good way to find out," he said. " Let's go talk to him."

They rode three abreast all the way down to where the balance of Dallas's DW men were holding perspiring, dusty and dishevelled banker Stubblefield. The moment they came up and halted Stubblefield broke into a loud denunciation of his captivity and denounced Curly Winters, the men with him, and even to a lesser extent, Dallas Wayne, because these rough-looking cowboys were his men. There were eight men around Stubblefield, counting Ben Willett, and every one of them sat there stonily patient waiting for the banker to get it all off his chest, and not for a moment did any of them take their eyes off the banker. Then, when Stubblefield finally began to tone down his protests, to gradually turn frightened and silent under those hostile stares, Ben Willett held up the package of money.

" What cowman were you goin' to deliver this thousand dollars to?" he mildly asked, and Stubblefield, who'd known Virginia City's constable a great many years, wasn't fooled for a moment by the mildness of Willett's tone.

" Well," he stammered. " What difference does that make, Ben? These DW riders are nothing but highwaymen; they stopped me without any right at all, took that money and—"

" George," cut in Willett in the same mild tone. " Cut it out. You lie to me an' so help me I'll drag you off that horse and stomp the waddin' out of you. Now, once more : who were you carryin' this money to?"

Stubblefield was not a brave man; resourceful yes, even clever in his own line of endeavour, but neither cleverness nor resourcefulness were going to be enough here and he knew it. His expression turned gustily defiant, then sly, and finally, under the unnerving looks of all those hostile faces, it crumpled and showed fear through oily sweat.

" I was absconding with it," he whispered.

Curly Winters and his companions exchanged looks. This was a new word to them. They were baffled by its meaning until Dallas said, " George, you weren't absconding with bank money. If you had been you wouldn't have taken just one thousand dollars. I happen to know for a fact that there's over thirteen thousand in your bank, in cash. Now George, I think I know where you were goin' with that money. So does Ben and the rest of these men. What I want to know first, is *why* you were takin' this money to him, and then I want to know where he's hiding."

"Dallas," gasped the banker, turning frantic eyes upon Wayne. "My duty is to protect the folks who have funds in my—"

"George," snapped Ben Willett, suddenly fierce and out of patience. "*Where is he!*"

Stubblefield's head jerked at the whiplash sound of Ben Willett's voice. He was copiously perspiring. He put Dallas in mind of a cornered animal the way he frantically flicked his glance around, the way he clutched his reins and writhed in his saddle. Finally he drooped, beaten and vanquished.

"He's hiding south of town another couple of miles waiting for me to bring him this money."

"Show us where," growled Ben Willett, surveying his long-time acquaintance with a gravelly look. Then he said, honestly curious, "What in hell ever possessed you, George?"

Stubblefield looked at Dallas when he answered. "I had to. I had no choice at all. He came to my house in the pit of the night and told me what had happened, that DW was after him now, and if I didn't fetch him the money he'd go back and kill Miss Smith, lay the blame upon Dallas Wayne, then stay and lead Circle S and everyone else who disliked Dallas—or who believed that story about him—in a bloodbath that'd level Virginia City and fill the cemetery."

Dallas considered Stubblefield for a long moment of quiet silence, then he lifted his rein-hand again. "Lead out," he ordered. "And George—he'll probably be watching, so when you think we're close enough, tell us an' we'll let you go ahead with the money."

Stubblefield eagerly nodded. "You're playing this smart," he retorted, some spirit returning to him. "Let him have the thousand; let him get away. Just make sure he leaves the country, that's all."

"No," dissented Dallas, "that's not all. But you do as you're told and leave the rest of it to us."

Willett made a rough gesture, his expression full of disillusionment and contempt. "Ride on, George. Do like Dallas said. Move out!"

Stubblefield rode loose and slack with Curly Winters on one side of him and another DW man on the other side of him. He didn't look around where the other horsemen were walking their animals, but if he had he'd have seen Dallas and Constable Willett in quiet conversation some hundred feet back.

"You believe him?" Willett asked.

Dallas shrugged. "I suppose so, Ben. When we get Sloan we can get his version also, then we'll know about what's true and what isn't."

Willett said, squinting acidly ahead at Stubblefield's back. "I believe him, Dallas. I've known him a long time—fifteen, eighteen years. He's not lyin', he just never had any head for bad situations, even as a young feller."

Curly left the van to return to Dallas's side and report that none of their men had come up with anything in their search. Then Curly lifted an arm and pointed off to the heat-hazed, far-distant southwest where some shimmering, barren grey abutments stood up off the plain. "Sloan's got his hideout down there, Stubblefield says. It's some kind of an old stone fort, or something."

Willett followed out the line Curly was indicating and

screwed up his face. " I know the spot. It wasn't really a fort; just a heap of stones against a backdrop of granite cliff where a bunch of emigrants forted-up to fight off a Piute attack in the early days." For a while Willett rode along gazing ahead at those bleak, barren hills and cliffs, then he said flintily. " Nobody but a damned fool would put his back to a sheer cliff when he's under attack."

" Sloan doesn't know yet he's under attack," exclaimed Curly. " Say, Constable; how far can he see from down there? Hadn't we better cut off pretty quick now?"

" Pretty quick," assented the lawman. " You go on back and put the fear o' gawd into George Stubblefield, because we got to turn him loose directly, an' if he rides up an' spills his guts to Sloan, there's a thousand miles of desert between here and California that Sloan can head out over, an' I'm damned if I got any stomach for *that* kind of a chase this time of year." Willett looked bleakly at Curly. " Make it damned good; you understand?"

Curly understood. He reined away and went loping on up where Stubblefield was poking along between two silent and watchful DW cowboys. Dallas watched Winters turn and start speaking to Stubblefield. He watched the banker's twisted, heat-reddened features, and he said aside to Ben : " I don't think George'll upset the applecart, Ben, but I'm sort of wondering whether or not we aren't being unnecessarily hard on him. After all, this isn't his environment, this world of frontier steel."

" Hard on him," grunted Willett, blackly scowling ahead. " I'd like to lay into him with an axe-handle. Why didn't the fool come to me when Sloan visited him? Why didn't he . . .?"

" I just told you, Ben. This isn't his environment.

He doesn't think like the rest of us do. He thought he was doing the right thing. He probably still thinks so."

17

STUBBLEFIELD HELD up his hand and the column halted. Ben Willett sat a moment with a pinched-down expression regarding those distant, heat-blurred rocky slopes. He begrudgingly nodded as Stubblefield, with Curly Winters riding beside him, came back and said, looking first at Willett then at less forbidding Dallas Wayne: " He'll be able to see us pretty quick now." Then Stubblefield sat waiting.

Willett said, without looking away from Ted Sloan's hideout hills, " George; if you're smart you won't tell him anything. Because I got a feelin' that if you *do* tell him, he's never goin' to believe you didn't bring us down here to get him." Willett swivelled his slitted eyes around. " He'll kill you, George, sure as you're sittin' there."

Stubblefield, though, had already thought this same thing, evidently, because he bobbed his head up and down. " All I ask is that you men don't hit him until I've ridden off. That's all I ask. Ben; the money?"

Willett fished out the brown-paper packet and handed it over. He didn't meet Stubblefield's gaze as he did this and as he afterwards said, " Maybe I ought to wish you good luck, George. Maybe when this is over I'll feel like doin' that, but right now I don't. Now go on. And George—you got a gun?"

Stubblefield nodded and patted a sagging coat-pocket. He looked once more at Dallas, then turned and without a rearward glance cut off the stage road heading at a walk southwesterly out through the sage and chaparral and other spiny desert-country underbrush. In all that empty, vast immensity, he looked very small, very insignificant.

Dallas watched him thoughtfully, wagged his head wryly and looked over at Willett. " You know the way," he said. " What's next?"

" Split up," replied Willett instantly, as though he'd already considered their strategy. " You take three men and keep goin' southward down the road until you're well past those hills, then *walk* your horses westward towards the hideout—*walk* 'em so you won't raise any dust—and cut him off southward. I'll take the rest of your crew and swing westward from where we now are. That ought to seal him off north and south, which are the two ways he'll probably try to escape after George gives him that damned money." Willett gazed around as though for a discussion, but none of the DW men said anything so he turned, jerked his head at the DW riders nearest him and started riding due westward.

Curly Winters lined up beside Dallas Wayne. So did the remaining riders. Without a word this party turned and continued on down-country. They loped for a half mile then walked their horses. It was a hot, tedious ride with a lot of uncertainty at the end of it, but by the time they'd covered a long two miles Dallas waved them off the road. They were by then southward of those westerly peaks and slopes. They were also perspiring hard, for this was the beginning of the big Nevada Desert. Not until they were a mile closer to the hills did one of them happen to glance northward and spot a dust-cloud far back.

For a while this held all their attention. Curly speculated that it was probably caused by one of the southbound stages. Another rider thought it was being caused by freight wagons travelling light. Dallas looked and gauged the distance, but beyond that he didn't speculate; he had something much more cogent upon his mind. Those onward, bleak and flintily barren lava-rock hillsides kept getting closer. By now, he was sure, George Stubblefield must be either very close to Sloan's hideout, or else he'd already arrived there.

There was no dust northward over against those distant hillsides and Dallas's band was raising no dust either. The jaws of Ben Willett's trap were inexorably closing.

Curly urged his horse a short distance ahead. He was riding straight up in his saddle with his head turning from left to right in a straining survey of the onward, dancing land. He abruptly hauled back and called sharply. He'd seen something moving in all that blurry emptiness. Dallas and the others pushed on up to also see. Curly pointed northward where a solitary horseman was jogging along.

Dallas sat still for a long time making certain, then he drew forth his Winchester and the men with him followed that example. " It's Sloan," Dallas said quietly. " I've got reason to recognise him when I see him."

Frank Webster's killer was a mile northward, but at the jogging rate he was travelling he'd be across in front of Dallas's crew within a few minutes.

Curly said, " Stubblefield sure didn't waste any time givin' him the money. Let's go."

They spread out now, though. Dallas and Curly, with big strong mounts, pushed straight on ahead to cut

Sloan off. The other DW men, without being told, slackened off, and in this manner helped establish a loose sort of mile-long skirmish line. Where the underbrush was thickest they made excellent time without booting their beasts out of a fast walk.

Sloan was riding straight up, but he didn't seem the least suspicious. He was alert, but whenever he looked around he concentrated upon the northward country, and this was his fatal mistake, because Dallas and Curly Winters got squarely across his route before he saw them. One moment Sloan was riding along watching his back-trail, the next moment he spotted sunlight off carbines dead ahead and had yanked his horse to a hard halt.

Dallas raised his voice. They were beyond gunshot of each other but in the thin, hushed atmosphere, his words carried well enough.

" Sloan; you're cut off in front and in back. Throw down your guns."

The 'breed threw down his guns but he went with them. He also yanked off his saddlebags too as he ducked and weaved deep into the sage. Curly swore a sizzling oath, dismounted and flagged for the farther-back DW rangeriders to also do the same. " Root him out," Curly sang out. " Fan out an' close in on him."

Dallas tied his horse, gestured for Curly to move off farther westward, then the pair of them began a slow, very careful advance through the sage and buckbrush. It was hot, dusty, tedious and dangerous work. Sloan could hear them pushing through the underbrush but they didn't hear him at all. Dallas, setting his course upon Sloan's abandoned, bewildered saddlehorse, came to a little clearing and moved out to cross it. A gun slammed its blasting snarl and dirt geysered up one foot behind

him. Dallas dived headfirst across the opening, landed
in a prickly clump of scrub, and rolled. Sloan slammed
two more carbine shots at him, both very close.

Curly opened up. He'd evidently caught sight of gun-
smoke. Southward the other DW men fired too, and
Dallas fervently hoped they weren't just making sound-
shots as he got gingerly clear of his thorny shield and
swivelled around seeking some sign of Sloan.

But the 'breed stopped firing and lay perfectly still.
He was proving himself an experienced desert-warrior.
Methodically Curly began to rake the underbrush where
Sloan had been. The other DW men, using Winters'
strategy as an example, also lay down a barrage of
ground-sluicing shots. Dallas did not believe Sloan could
weather that leaden storm without moving and he was
correct. The underbrush began to quiver where a craw-
ling man was desperately trying to get clear of those
searching bullets. Dallas raised up onto one knee,
shouldered his carbine and waited. The movement halted
less than two hundred feet eastward of him. Sloan had
either dropped down feeling secure or else he'd en-
countered one of those little clearings which interspersed
the underbrush-growth.

Dallas fired.

A man's hat sailed out over the sage and a frantic
beating set the brush to quivering again. An answering
gunshot came back almost before Dallas could drop
down and crawl away. It flung grit into his face and
eyes making him drop his carbine and dig at both eyes
with his fists. His battered, cracked lips were already
bleeding and the bruises on his face from Phil Billings's
fists burnt with a steady pain, but this fresh agony made
these sensations pale into insignificance. Tears poured
down his cheeks partially clearing his sight. Eastward, his

rangeriders were closing in on Sloan. One of them called sharply when he sighted movement. This man and his companions poured a galling fusillade into the sage.

Curly, too far westward, came working his way along until he found Dallas with tears streaming down from his bloodshot eyes. Winters immediately dropped down to lend a hand but Dallas shook his head; the worst of the pain was past now, and gradually his sight was improving. He drew his hand-gun, twisted half around, beckoned for Winters to follow, and went ahead through the brush straight towards the place where Sloan was fiercely returning that eastward gunfire. If there had ever been reluctant reservations in Dallas Wayne's mind about the punishment for Sloan—and there had been, although he hadn't said so in front of his riders—there were none now. He and his rangeboss, separated by less than a hundred feet, worked through the underbrush until, close enough to begin a nearby search, they were suddenly forced to drop flat as a party of shooting, howling riders swept down recklessly from the north. Ben Willett and the balance of the DW crew, drawn swiftly from their up-country sortie by gunfire, came bursting upon the scene.

Dallas felt like swearing. Bullets were slashing all around him through the sage. Someone did indignantly howl from southward a-ways, and Willett's gritty bawl ordered the men with him to cease firing. At the precise moment Ben gave that order, something lean and dark sailed over a sage clump and landed squarely atop Dallas Wayne. He had only a fraction of a second to see Ted Sloan's darkly twisted face, then Sloan was clubbing at him with his .45.

Dallas felt the wild stab of pain where the steel gun barrel smashed into his back. He rolled frantically and lashed out with his own gun. Sloan, evidently with no premonition that Dallas was where he'd meant to land deep in the underbrush, nevertheless reacted almost spontaneously. He was twisting around and cocking his gun almost before he struck the ground. Curly Winters, clawing forward at those sounds, caught sight of Sloan and fired. He missed.

Dallas, with no time to aim, with scarcely time enough to fling himself clear, was nearly deafened when Sloan fired. The bullet ploughed up a handful of dirt no more than three inches from Dallas's left. Sloan, fighting to spring upright and re-cock his .45, saw Dallas's muzzle bearing straight upon him from a distance of less than ten feet, and froze. Dallas fired.

Curly Winters, jumping over brush clumps to get closer, was struck head-on by Sloan's hurtling body. Under the murderous impact of such close-range, Dallas's bullet had caught Sloan squarely in the centre of the chest with the full force of a sledge-hammer blow. It knocked him backwards straight into Curly. The pair of them went down in a heap with Curly swearing and lashing out at a dead man.

Dallas rolled over, got both legs squarely set, and stood up. There was no need for a second shot. He bent, caught Sloan, yanked him clear of Curly, and let go. Winters got up spitting dirt, still swearing. He had been more than just bowled over, he'd also been badly shaken to find that he'd been desperately grappling with a corpse.

There was no more gunfire, but for almost a full minute the silence remained unbroken. Finally, a DW man called out in a rising voice asking if Sloan was dead. Curly said that he was. Northward too, men on horseback pushed through the brush. When the entire

band was assembled there, only one man was missing—
George Stubblefield.

Ben Willett dismounted stiffly, put up his gun, knelt
and studied Sloan in total silence. When he afterwards
regained his feet he turned and cast a narrowed glance
over towards the road eastward. He muttered softly.
" Now who the hell is this comin'?"

They all turned. It was Burlette Smith with Harry
Lyon beside her and all the rest of her Circle S men
riding bunched up around her.

Ben swore. " Who set her loose?" he snarled.

Dallas put forth a hand to delay Willett's progress
towards those oncoming riders. Old Ben was bristling.
" Let it go for now," Dallas said. " We got what we came
here for, Ben."

Up close where they halted, the Circle S men parted
and pushed a wrinkled, limp and grey-faced rider out
ahead. It was George Stubblefield; he craned over with
rounded eyes to stare at sprawled and lifeless Ted Sloan.
" You got him," Stubblefield whispered. " You got him."

Dallas went back for his Winchester. He then walked
deliberately over where Burlette had dismounted, halted,
leaned upon his carbine and stonily regarded her. " Add
jailbreak to the rest of it," he said, and shook his head.

She didn't answer, she instead turned, took down a
canteen from her saddle and handed it to him. She then
removed a little silken neckerchief and offered him that
too. " Your face is like raw beefsteak," she said. " This
should cool it. And yes—I broke out; with the help of
Harry and my other men, but not to do whatever you're
thinking. I wanted to help rectify all the wrong Sloan
and Billings—and I—have done. Mister Wayne; ride
back with me. I'd like to make you a proposition."

Ben Willett and Curly Winters came up, halted and

glared. Dallas headed off any additional unpleasantness. "Fetch my horse," he said to Curly, and began bathing his face. "Ben; Miss Smith an' I're goin' to ride back now. You have any objections?"

Willett kept on glaring, first at Burlette, then at her wooden-faced riders. "You fellers let that danged fee-lawyer out too?" he demanded of the Circle S men.

Burlette shook her head. "No, Constable. He's still in your jailhouse. If you'll let me I'd like to make restitution for whatever—"

"You," broke in grim Ben Willett, "go on an' ride back with Dallas. And if he don't skin you alive on the way I'm goin' to when we get to town, girl. I knew your pappy and your uncles; believe me, if they was here right now they'd do the same thing. No go on—get out of my sight."

Willett turned back where the DW men were tying Ted Sloan across a saddlehorse. He halted though, and twisted to watch Dallas Wayne and Burlette Smith mount their horses. Curly Winters came shambling along after delivering Dallas's mount to him and Ben said, "Curly; you reckon he could make that danged woman into a decent, law-abidin' female-wife sort of girl?"

Curly was nonplussed. He craned around as Dallas and Burlette rode off and let his jaw sag. Such an incredible notion had never occurred to him. It was like being doused with ice-water.

When they reached the stage road and turned northward Burlette handed an oilskin packet across to Dallas. "That's what made the difference," she said as Dallas took the packet and pushed it inside his sweat-limp and torn shirt. "But at first I didn't understand what you were trying to tell me with those papers."

"It's simple enough," Dallas said. "A man named

Dallas Wayne *did* murder a Yankee courier at Sabine Pass, but as you saw, ma'am, I served throughout the war, not in Hood's Brigade, but in Jubal Early's army. The name Dallas isn't unusual among Texans, and the name Wayne isn't unusual anywhere. In one sentence, ma'am, there were two Dallas Wayne's."

"And that rider who thought he'd recognised you as the one who'd killed that courier . . ."

"Miss Burlette, that was almost twenty years ago. Anyone could make that same mistake an' I reckon it's been made a lot of times since those days, even among old comrades."

"Mister Wayne; what can I do . . .?"

He smiled. "We'll talk about that over supper. All right?"

She smiled straight into his eyes. "All right."